'You do not

one, do you?

Kit decided sile the best policy—there was nothing she could say.

'I am clearly the lesser of two evils and it is a long time since I have been cast in such a role——' Gerard's glittering gold eyes moved swiftly over her '—especially by such a beautiful woman.'

'You said you didn't find me attractive . . .'

The deep voice was unrepentant. 'I lied!'

Dear Reader

The new year is a time for resolutions and here at Mills & Boon we will continue to give you the best romances we possibly can. We're sure the year's books will live up to your expectations! This month we hope to shake off the winter chills by taking you to some wonderful exotic locations—Morocco, the Bahamas and the Caribbean. Closer to home, this is the time of year when we celebrate love and lovers, with St Valentine's Day. Which of our heroes would you like to spend the day with? Until next month,

The Editor

Helen Brooks lives in Northamptonshire and is married with three children. As she is a committed Christian, busy housewife and mother, her spare time is at a premium but her hobbies include reading, swimming, gardening and walking her two energetic, inquisitive and very endearing young dogs. Her long-cherished aspiration to write became a reality when she put pen to paper on reaching the age of forty, and sent the result off to Mills & Boon.

Recent titles by the same author:

KNIGHT IN BLACK VELVET
THE SULTAN'S FAVOURITE
WEB OF DARKNESS

DARK OASIS

BY

HELEN BROOKS

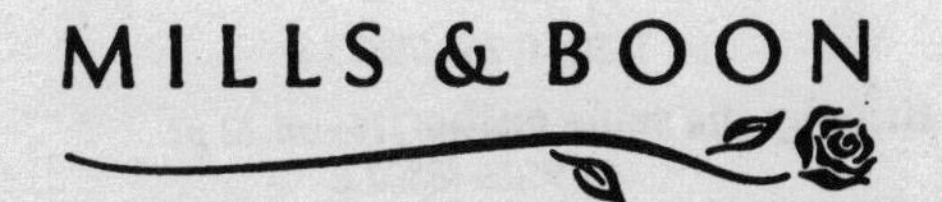

MILLS & BOON LIMITED
ETON HOUSE, 18-24 PARADISE ROAD
RICHMOND, SURREY TW9 1SR

First published in Great Britain 1994 by Mills & Boon Limited

This edition 1995

ISBN 0 263 78873 3

Set in Times Roman 11½ on 12 pt.
01-9502-48800 C

Made and printed in Great Britain

CHAPTER ONE

'KIT! Where on earth are you? Everyone's absolutely frantic here and David's been tearing his hair out. As well he might! Are you all right, for goodness' sake?'

'I'm fine.' Kit took a long, deep breath. She didn't even want to hear David's name. 'It's over between us. Did he tell you?'

'Yes.' Her friend's voice was scathing. 'He's such a fool, Kit, he always has been, even if he *is* my brother. To mess about with Virginia of all people—*Virginia*! Never has a name been more un-apt, or at least the first six letters.'

'Emma...' Kit closed her eyes briefly and prayed for her voice to sound cool and calm despite her racing heart. 'I don't want to discuss it. I found them in bed and our engagement is over. That's it. End of story. Now, I've arranged for my half of the rent for our flat to be paid——'

'But where are you?' Emma interrupted urgently. 'You wouldn't do anything silly, would you?'

'Of course not!' Her voice had risen and she breathed deeply before speaking again, her tone a few decibels lower. 'I'm having a short holiday in the sun to think where I'm going to go from here, that's all. I'll contact you in a week or so, OK? Bye for now and take care.'

She put down the receiver and leant back against the small booth in the hotel lobby, shaking violently. The brief phone call had brought David vividly to mind and it was as though his face were there in front of her, his mouth a snarl as she had faced him in the doorway of the flat they were buying together for their intended marriage four months away, Virginia's naked body hidden from her sight now behind the closed bedroom door that he had slammed shut as he had raced after her. 'Damn well listen to me!' He had pulled the towelling dressing-gown more tightly round him as her large grey eyes flicked disgustedly over his rumpled appearance.

'There is no point, David.' She was working on automatic, she knew it, but she blessed the shock that was keeping her from disintegrating in front of him. 'And I think this belongs to you.' As she deliberately removed the diamond engagement ring from her finger and held it out to him, his pale good-looking face flushed red, a hint of unease and panic replacing the aggressive bravado with which he had met her stunned face.

'Don't be so stupid,' he spat angrily. 'You're not throwing me over because of that?' He flung back a contemptuous hand towards the closed bedroom door through which she had walked so innocently minutes before. 'I was just easing myself; she was available—Kit!' He caught hold of her arm and she was made to turn without a word. 'Kit, you can't mean it? We're getting married, we've got this flat, furniture, everything——'

'Keep it.' Let me get out of here with a little dignity, she prayed desperately. 'Keep it all.' She was tall at five feet ten, her slender figure carrying an unmistakable air of cool composure, and she had never been more glad of it as she met him eye to eye, her mouth curling with contempt. 'I wouldn't marry you now if you were the last man on earth.'

The torrent of abuse that followed her as she made her escape polluted the very air, mixing with the picture on the screen of her mind of Virginia's sprawled naked limbs beneath David's heaving thrusting body, and now, as Kit relived the sickening episode, she felt the need to breathe in some fresh clean air. As she left the pleasant coolness of the air-conditioned building and stepped into the Moroccan heat, it was like stepping into an oven, the iridescent blue sky shimmering with heat. *Casablanca*. Kit squared her slim shoulders as she walked towards the little red convertible she had hired for her stay, pushing the bitter hurt and painful humiliation back into the closed box in her mind. She'd face that, and the tangles that would undoubtedly ensue over the little design business Emma, David and herself had started eighteen months ago, later. Enough of licking her wounds; today she was going to explore, and if tonight in the quiet of her room she cried hot, angry tears again, well . . . only she would know.

She travelled southward along the Atlantic coast from Casablanca making for Essaouira, meaning small fortress in Arabic. The hotel manager had fired her interest, explaining that the large harbour in the town had been used for thousands of years, ancient Romans frequently visiting to obtain a brilliant colouring material produced from shellfish and used for dyeing their robes purple. Ancient cannons still lined the main street and, after wandering its length, she turned into a quieter area. But, then, just as she felt the hairs on the back of her neck prickle a warning about the footsteps behind her, a heavy blow on the side of her head turned the light into splintered glass, and as her shoulder-bag was wrenched from her arm she fell. Fell into a hot blackness that seemed to race up from the dusty ground to consume her.

She came out of the buzzing whirl of unconsciousness slowly, very slowly, aware of a sick pounding in her head that dominated all her senses and made her limbs like lead. 'Can you hear me? Try and open your eyes.' A deep male voice and a cool hand on her burning forehead registered on her bruised mind, but as her eyelids fluttered in obedience the piercing light drove them instantly shut. 'No matter. I am going to lift you now but you are perfectly safe. Do you understand me?' She couldn't reply, and in the next instant she was being carried. She knew she ought to try and open her eyes again, to speak, but somehow it was so much easier to slip back into that soft enveloping darkness . . .

'Try and hang in there this time.'

'What?' As she forced her heavy lids open, the cool shadowed room made it easier to fix her wavering gaze on the hard male face in front of her.

'You have been slipping in and out of consciousness for the last few minutes.'

He was dark and magnificently male, his voice the one she had heard before. The accent teased her mind. French? Italian perhaps?

'Just lie still and try to concentrate on my face only until the dizziness stops,' he continued softly. 'OK?'

It was more than OK. If Michelangelo's *David* was beautiful, this man's face was stunning. His gleaming hair was a thick tawny brown worn unusually long, almost down to his shoulders. High, hard cheekbones, straight nose and sensual, almost cruel lips below eyes that were the same tawny gold-brown as his hair completed a picture of such aggressive, vibrant masculinity that Kit felt her toes begin to curl.

But who was he? And where was she? And why did she feel so desperately ill? 'Please . . .' As she tried to struggle into a sitting position on the wide leather couch on which she was lying, he moved quickly, his body carrying the same powerful grace as a beautiful wild animal.

'I said lie still.' His voice was firm and cool. 'You've received a nasty blow on the head so just take it easy.'

'I have . . . ?' As her voice trailed away on a little gulp, she felt hot tears of weakness and pain prick against her eyelids seconds before he spoke again.

'And do not dissolve on me, not yet.' He fixed her with that hard tawny gaze that reminded her of the piercing stare of one of the big cats watching its intended prey. 'I need to know your name, hotel, something. You are a tourist, I think?' His voice was cool and steady and quite unemotional.

'A tourist?' Her tongue felt too big for her mouth. 'I don't know.'

A tourist? The panic that had been at the back of her mind ever since she had opened her eyes began to claw at her throat with strangling fingers. She could be a tourist. She could be anything. She didn't remember.

'Just relax.' He saw the naked horror in her eyes and recognised it for what it was. 'You're clearly concussed, which is not surprising in the circumstances. Unfortunately the animal that did this to you also took your bag, so we have no identification to help us. I was hoping when you awoke you could provide a few answers but as it is——' he shrugged massive shoulders slowly '—the police will have to sort it.'

As he leant towards her she cowered instinctively into the bulk of the couch, flushing as he eyed her sardonically with cool raised eyebrows before wiping her face and mouth gently with a damp perfumed cloth. 'As I said, relax.'

He stood up from his crouching position at her side and it registered on her just how tall he was, well over six feet, inches over, and with a powerful hard frame that would win first prize in any Mr Universe competition. 'My name is Gerard Dumont, by the way,' he added lazily as he folded muscled arms to stand staring down at her impassively. French. Yes, she should have known. 'And you are...?'

'I...' Her voice trailed away as her eyes widened. 'My name... I don't know it.' She raised agonised eyes to the gold of his. 'I don't know who I am.'

'This is not a difficulty; do not panic.' The pronunciation of his words and correct English in that broken accent was incredibly attractive, she thought faintly as she struggled for composure. 'The bump will heal and then you will remember.' He smiled suddenly and she drew in a hard short breath of air. He was something. He *really* was something. Did he know the effect he had on women? She looked into the darkly tanned handsome face silently, mesmerised by her own unaccustomed helplessness and vulnerability and the frightening loss of memory. She had to try to remember. She must remember something. 'The police are on their way, incidentally.' He eyed her lazily. 'It would seem you were perverse enough to be, how you say, mugged at the same time as a rather large jewellery robbery was under way in the middle of the town. Needless to say, you were not considered the immediate priority.'

'Oh.' Her head felt as though it was going to explode any minute. 'Where am I?' It was the ultimate stage response to fit the situation, but for the life of her she couldn't think of a less unsubtle rejoinder.

'In my office.' The gold eyes narrowed a little. 'Can you not remember anything at all? Look down at your clothes; they may produce a spark. It would be preferable to the mountain of questions the police may ask. Subtlety is not their strong point here.'

She glanced down at her legs stretched out in front of her encased in light white cotton trousers, the cut impeccable, and tried to focus her whirling thoughts into some sort of order. Her feet were shod in slender coffee-coloured sandals that matched her waist-length blouse exactly, and again she noticed that both items seemed expensive. Well, fine. She obviously wasn't destitute, but who on earth *was* she?

'No.' She sank back against the couch and shut her eyes again. 'I'm sorry.'

When the police arrived a few minutes later she discovered one thing; she couldn't speak the language. Fortunately the two police officers seemed quite fluent in English but she couldn't tell them much, repeating the same thing over and over again until her head spun.

'I think the lady needs to see a doctor,' Gerard cut into the interrogation after a time, his hard face autocratic.

'Do I have to go with them?' She looked up at him, her large grey eyes suddenly terrified at the thought of leaving the only person she had any knowledge of, albeit a slight one, in this strange country.

'You will be quite safe.' His tone was slightly abrupt, preoccupied, and she noticed as he spoke that he glanced at the heavy gold watch on his wrist before meeting her eyes, a small frown wrinkling his brow.

'I suppose I will.' She wasn't aware her voice was sharp, but he couldn't have made it more clear that she was an awkward inconvenience and everything in her rose up in immediate opposition. 'You must be a very busy man, Mr Dumont; please don't let me keep you. Thank you for your kindness.' The words were grateful, the slight edge to her voice anything but. And then he looked at her, really looked at her, for the first time and grey eyes met gold, the former defiant, proud and very dismissive and the latter narrowed with surprise. 'Have you finished for now?' She spoke directly to the older policeman, a plump hard-faced individual in his middle fifties with eyes of stone. 'Then if you wouldn't mind taking me to the nearest hospital, we'll sort things out from there.'

Was she used to directing people like this? she asked herself faintly as she stood gingerly on her feet, her head thudding. It didn't feel unnatural so she supposed she must be. She felt terrified, sick and desperately helpless but this man Gerard had made it perfectly plain he didn't want to get involved, and she was blowed if she'd beg—she'd sort it out herself. She suddenly had the feeling she'd been doing that for a long, long time. Tears prickled under her eyelashes again and she blinked them away quickly. She'd cry later.

'Look.' Gerard steadied her with his arm round her waist as she stood swaying in the cool, air-conditioned room. 'Please do not misunderstand me. I have an important appointment, that is all. I——'

'Thank you, Mr Dumont.' She moved out of his hold on trembling legs and offered him a slim hand, her chin high. 'I hope you won't be late...' As the blackness took over again she just heard him growl something in muttered French that sounded incredibly rude as she fell, and then there was nothing, nothing but this soft enveloping darkness that cushioned her buzzing racing senses in the thick blanket of unconsciousness.

She awoke to the sterile neutrality of a small white room that smelt of antiseptic and carbolic, and the realisation that she had tried to surface several times before from the crazy world she had inhabited for the last little while, a world of whirling images and alien voices all of which were dominated by grinding, unrelenting pain in her head. But there was no pain now. She moved her head slightly on the hard pillow and winced as a flash of something hot spiked into her brain. Well, not if she kept still.

There was a buzzer connected to a long wire lying on the white counterpane next to her right hand, and she pressed it carefully before her eyes moved to the small narrow window at the end of the room. The grey light filtering through the louvre blinds suggested it was either dusk or dawn and she realised with a little dart of anxiety that she had no idea which it was. Or *where* she was. Or—and here the thought became a hard thudding in her chest—who she was. She shut her eyes tightly and prayed for calm. She remembered falling in that hot dusty street and hitting her head on the rough jagged kerb. She remembered being helped into a cool shaded room and she remembered... Her thoughts stopped abruptly. Yes, she remembered Gerard Dumont. And then, as if her mind had conjured him up, the creaking of the door brought her eyes open and there he was, closely followed by a small nurse.

'Ah, you are awake.' The smile was as devastating as she recalled and her limbs turned to water. 'The doctor thought a few hours' sleep would put you to rights.'

'Did he?' She glanced round carefully as she hitched herself up slightly in the bed, finding that if she moved slowly her head still belonged to her. 'I'm in hospital?'

'Just an overnight stay,' he said coolly. 'And do not start imagining the worst. You have concussion and——' He stopped abruptly.

'And?' But then the nurse took over, popping a thermometer in her mouth which stopped further conversation as she took her blood pressure with bright impersonal efficiency.

He leant back against the wall as the nurse went about her ministrations, arms crossed and big body relaxed as he watched her with tawny narrowed eyes. She found his presence incredibly unsettling, and as her cheeks began to burn so did her temper. Surely he didn't have the right to be in her room like this? This was a hospital, for goodness' sake. And she didn't even know the man. She'd be having a bed-bath next to complete the indignities! And he *had* wanted to be rid of her.

As soon as the thermometer was out of her mouth she spoke carefully, her eyes veiled. 'I appreciate your help, Mr Dumont, but perhaps it would be better if you left now? I don't want to inconvenience you further. I'm fine and this is a hospital, when all's said and done——'

'A private nursing home actually,' he corrected coolly, levering himself off the wall, with a nod and a smile to the nurse as she left, and walking lazily over to the side of the bed to survey her with an expressionless face. 'And as I am paying the bill, I do not foresee a problem.' He knew exactly how she felt about him, she realised with a little shiver.

'You're...?' She stared aghast at the tall figure watching her so closely. 'But why? There are hospitals here, aren't there? I mean——'

'I know what you mean.' He smiled, but there was no warmth in the twist of his mouth. 'And before that active little imagination runs riot, let me assure you that I have no designs on your body.' There was something almost contemptuous in the gold eyes as they ran over her slender form under the white bedclothes. 'I prefer my women with a little more meat on their bones and definitely more submissive.'

I bet you do, she thought angrily as her eyes sparked. I just bet you do. And I'm glad you know I don't like you!

'Nevertheless you asked for my protection before you passed out at my feet, and that is exactly what I have given you, so please do not agitate yourself.' The hard gaze was piercing as it roved consideringly over her hot cheeks. 'Also the hospital here is perhaps not quite what you were used to in—England? Do you come from England?'

'I think so.' She stared at him as the anger drained and the enormity of her problem took hold again. 'I must do. I look English, don't I?'

'To the tips of your feet,' he assured her gravely. 'And your demeanour is all English.' Somehow she felt it wasn't a compliment and again her temper was ignited.

'What exactly does that mean?' she asked hotly.

'Cucumber-cool and twice as self-contained,' he said smoothly, the dark tanned face slightly amused at her indignation. 'You do not like this description?'

'I can live with it,' she returned shortly, and then felt immediately ashamed of her ingratitude. But then...she didn't trust him, not one little bit. Why would a complete stranger pay for her to be cared for in a private hospital anyway? There was a catch here, she just knew it. Or was she generally just distrustful of people and men in particular? she asked herself silently. She didn't know, she just didn't know. The panic rose hot and fierce.

'Is there a mirror anywhere?' she asked weakly, as she glanced up from her musing to find the strange gold eyes intent on her face.

'You look delightful——'

'I don't care what I *look* like,' she said sharply before wincing as the pain shot through her head again. 'I just want to see...to see who I am,' she finished miserably.

'Of course.' Suddenly the hard face softened. 'I will call the nurse to take you to the bathroom in case you should feel a little unwell again, yes?' He paused as he walked over to the door and turned again, his eyes searching her white face slowly. 'You *will* remember soon, little one, have no fear about that. The police are making enquiries and soon someone will notice you are missing.'

'But perhaps I'm here by myself?' she said weakly. 'Perhaps I've rented a place even? I could have.' She stared at him, her eyes wide and the pupils unnaturally dilated. 'I could have a child waiting for me, pets, anything. I don't *know*, do I?'

'This is true,' he said gravely, 'but if you try to remember too hard I think it will be even more difficult.'

'That's all very well for you to say,' she said tightly. 'You aren't me, are you? Not that this would have happened to a man, I suppose,' she added bitterly.

'You think the male sex is impervious to being attacked?' he asked quietly, his eyes narrowing at the look of resentment darkening her face.

'Not necessarily, no.' Her eyes met his again. 'But you sure as hell have things your own way most of the time. Women are just appendages of a man's ego, that's all...' Her voice trailed away as she realised what she had said. What had made her feel like that? She felt something large and dark looming in the background and shut her eyes tightly. She had to remember.

'I will fetch the nurse.' She didn't look up as he spoke, and as the door shut behind him she opened her eyes slowly as she sank back against the pillows. This was a living nightmare and one from which there was no awakening. She put her arms round her middle and hugged herself tightly as the panic clawed at her stomach, sending it churning sickeningly. She was exposed, vulnerable, helpless... Her heart began to thud crazily, and when the little nurse knocked and entered in the next instant she could have kissed her, so pleased was she to have another human being in the room to counter the monsters in her mind.

She was quite steady on her feet as she made her way along to the bathroom on the arm of the nurse, and after insisting that the small Moroccan girl wait outside and promising twice not to lock the door, she walked gingerly over to the cloudy square mirror above the small white washbasin and peered at herself with bated breath.

A pair of large, grey, darkly lashed eyes stared back at her nervously and then continued their inspection of the reflection. Small, straight nose, a somewhat wide generous mouth, she noted wanly, and all set in a clear skin that was real peaches and cream. Thick, sleek, chestnut-brown hair with more than a touch of red in its silky depths gave an explanation of the freckles scattered across her nose, and the short bob was expertly cut, complementing the fine features and upward tilt of her chin. Altogether reasonably attractive, although she would never win any beauty contests, she thought slowly, and it didn't mean a thing to her. It could have been the face of anyone, the face of a stranger. *What was she going to do*? She sat down on the loo and put her head between her hands as she tried to think. She was all alone in a foreign country... or at least she thought it was a foreign country. For all she knew, she lived here. She groaned softly. Surely the police would find out something soon? They had to, this was horrific. And that man, Gerard Dumont. Why did she have this feeling that she had to be rid of him at the earliest opportunity? That he spelt danger with a capital D? Could she trust her instincts? They were the only thing she had right now.

He was waiting in her room when she returned with the nurse, his big frame stretching lazily as he stood up at their approach, his whole demeanour casual and relaxed but his eyes hawklike on her face as she passed, although he said not a word as the nurse settled her back into bed.

'I fetch the breakfast, yes?' The small girl smiled cheerfully. 'And then you feel a million dollars with plenty of zow?'

I wouldn't bank on it, Kit thought silently as she smiled a dutiful response as the nurse left the room.

'The police phoned.' Gerard Dumont settled himself back on the stool by her bed that he had vacated a minute before, and she raised her eyes reluctantly to his. 'No luck yet, unfortunately; it would appear you are the mystery girl. The doctor will be along shortly to examine you, but if all is as he thinks there is no reason why you cannot leave this morning.'

'To go where?' she asked blankly as her mind raced. Was there a British embassy near here? But then she wasn't even sure she *was* English.

'Well, I do have an idea there as it happens,' he drawled slowly, lifting dark brows as he watched her carefully, his face cynical and cool. 'But maybe it would be better for you to eat your breakfast first and——'

'I would prefer to hear anything you have to say right now,' she said firmly, her chin setting at a determined angle that brought an amused gleam into the glittering gold-brown eyes trained on her face.

'As you wish.' He stood up abruptly, walking over to the small narrow window and lifting the blind aside so that a shaft of sunlight spilled into the austere room, catching a million tiny particles in its radiant light. 'I was going to suggest that it would seem logical for you to remain resting somewhere until either you regain your memory or the police find out who you are, yes?'

'I suppose so.' She glanced at the broad back warily. 'And?'

'And that would pose a problem, or at least an embarrassment, as you have no money that I know of?' He turned to face her, his eyes slits of gold light.

'You know I haven't.' She stared back, hard. 'But I can assure you that once all this is sorted out I will reimburse you for every penny you've spent——'

'Do not be ridiculous.' This time his voice was harsh, and she blinked twice before opening her mouth to respond, but he continued swiftly. 'The money is incidental, as I am sure you are aware. I was merely stating facts.'

'Well, now you've stated them I still don't understand——'

'It would seem practical for you to be my guest until you are recovered sufficiently to take charge of your own affairs,' he said expressionlessly. 'There are several guest-rooms at my home in Marrakesh, and as I am a prominent and well-known figure in business circles I am sure the police would be happy to——'

'*You must be joking!*' Tact and diplomacy fled out of the window as she reared up in the narrow bed like a small lioness. 'You must think I was born yesterday, Mr Dumont! So that's what this has all been about, the private room and so on! Well, if you expect me to pay for my expenses in the fashion that is as old as time, you can forget it, mister! I know your sort—believe me, you're far from being unique! I'd rather spend the next few days, weeks or months in a prison cell if necessary compared to what you're suggesting. Just what do you think I am——?'

'I think you are a very absurd young lady.' The icy voice cut short her passionate outburst as though with a knife. 'Impolite, churlish, ridiculous... Need I go on?' He was angry; she couldn't believe *how* angry. 'Do you seriously think that I am so short of female companions that I have to spirit one away to my home—is that it?' He wasn't shouting, in fact his voice was very controlled and infinitely cutting. 'If you want me to be brutal, I do not find you sexually attractive at all. The offer was one of friendship, from one member of the human race to another in distress. That is all. *That is all.*' He glared at her and took a long deep pull of air before continuing. 'Now you have made your feeling perfectly clear, and so I will—— '

What he would or would not do they never found out because at that moment Kit's control finally snapped. The flood of tears and sensation of utter and absolute desolation blinded and deafened her to everything but her own misery, and as she raised her hands to cover her face, her body shaking helplessly, she could hear the sound of her own wailing but could do nothing to control it.

'*Mon dieu...*' His voice was a low growl but the next moment she had been lifted wholesale out of the bed and on to his lap as he sat down on the ruffled covers, holding her tight as he swayed back and forth as one did soothing a devastated child, his voice low and soft now and speaking a crooning stream of endearments in French of which she understood not a word but found infinitely comforting to her terrified mind. And she *was* terrified, she acknowledged faintly as the hard male bulk of him banished the frantic fear for a time. Nothing, *nothing* could be worse than this monstrous, gut-wrenching dread that she would never remember who she was again, that she would be left in this strange, alien half-world where even her own face was that of a stranger, with no memories, no recollection of a past life and with only an empty, uncertain future to look forward to.

CHAPTER TWO

QUITE when she began to find Gerard Dumont's closeness disturbing rather than comforting she wasn't sure. It might have been something to do with the warm male fragrance emanating from the massive frame, a mixture of spicy aftershave and a faint lemony smell, or it could have been the controlled power in the huge body enfolding hers, or even the sound of his voice, deep and seductively attractive as he murmured in his native tongue. Whatever, as the storm of weeping passed she began to feel acutely uncomfortable and vaguely threatened. But there was another emotion there too, one that made her skin tingle and her stomach tighten with a dull ache she didn't recognise.

'I'm sorry.' As she made to move off his lap he let her go instantly, his eyes searching as they washed over her face.

'Have you any idea where all that hostility comes from?' he asked levelly as he stood up and drew back the covers for her to climb back into bed. 'What has happened to make you feel so threatened by the male species?'

'Threatened?' She stared at him wide-eyed, horrified he could read her so easily. 'I don't feel threatened——'

'Yes, you do.' He eyed her impassively and she was conscious of his great height again as he gestured towards the bed. 'Get in. The nurse will be bringing your breakfast in a moment.'

'I don't feel threatened.' She ignored his instructions with obstinate determination. 'This has all just been unsettling, surely you can understand that?'

'I told you that the doctor confirmed concussion?' His voice was low and moderate but with an underlying thread of steel. 'And undoubtedly you have a secondary complication resulting in amnesia. However...' He paused and gestured towards the bed again, his mouth thinning as she still refused to acknowledge the command. 'However, the blow to your head was not severe enough for this continued loss of memory.'

'Are you saying I'm making it up?' she asked hotly as her skin burnt with anger. 'I can assure you——'

'Of course I am not saying that,' he interrupted sharply, 'and for my sake if not yours please get yourself into this damn bed. I do not relish the prospect of picking you up off the floor again and you look distinctly feeble.'

'Thank you *very* much,' she intoned furiously, as sheer temper enabled her to march across the room and climb into the bed more quickly than she would have thought possible in view of her trembling legs and throbbing head.

'What I *am* saying, or rather what the doctor is saying, is that there is something that is causing you to block out your past,' Gerard said slowly. 'Something that you do not wish to remember, something that would cause you great pain——'

'Now it's you who's being ridiculous,' she said quickly as a spark of something blindingly menacing flashed across her mind before sinking back into her subconscious. 'You are,' she continued faintly as the dark shadow crept back into that inner mind. 'I had an accident, I was attacked——'

'Of course you were,' he said softly, 'no one is disputing that, but the accident has merely allowed your mind to hide behind this incident, take refuge if you like.'

'No, I *don't* like.' She glared at him, far more shaken than she would admit. 'Are you saying I'm unbalanced, is that it?'

'*Mon dieu*...' The exclamation was made in the form of a curse. 'I have never met such an awkward, difficult——'

'And where is this wonderful doctor who has made such a profound diagnosis without even telling me?' she asked angrily. 'Do I actually get to see him or what?'

'After breakfast.' The nurse had just entered carrying a loaded tray, her bright black eyes flashing from one angry face to the other before concentrating on the food with lowered gaze and a tactfully bland face. 'I'm joining you, is that all right?'

'Fine; you're paying after all.' She regretted the coarseness of the retort as soon as it left her lips and raised her eyes instantly to his face, her mouth trembling. 'I'm sorry, that was awful. *I'm* being awful, it's just that——'

'Eat your breakfast.' His tone was firm but not unkind, the hard handsome face expressionless.

'I don't think I could eat anything——'

'You will, if I have to force-feed you every mouthful,' he replied softly, still in the same firm, emotionless voice.

She glared at him angrily and then met the full force of the startlingly cat-like gaze that suddenly told her she would lose this particular battle if she persevered. She gulped, gave him a blazing scowl that could have melted stone at thirty paces and gave in, discovering as she bit into a warm crusty croissant that she was hungry after all.

He didn't speak again until she was finishing her second cup of coffee, and when he did she jumped so violently that most of the semi-hot liquid left in the cup splashed on to the white covers. 'Have you made a decision?'

'A decision?' She raised her eyes to meet his, knowing exactly what he meant but playing for time as her mind raced back and forth seeking a solution to the impossible situation.

He shook his tawny head slowly as he stretched lazily on the stool, his face dark and sardonic and his mouth twisted with cynical amusement. 'Yes, a decision,' he intoned drily. 'And do not insult my intelligence by asking what about. I really could not take that.' As he stood up his bulk seemed to fill the small room, dominating the white surroundings with a menacing energy that suddenly made her breathless. 'I have to go. I have an appointment at nine.'

'Oh, right . . .' She raised a hand to her face to brush back a lock of hair and was annoyed to see it was shaking, and then felt doubly humiliated when she saw Gerard had noticed it too.

'Do I terrify you so much?' His voice was soft, and as her eyes flashed to his she saw he was not smiling, that all amusement and mockery had left the hard masculine face. 'I do not wish to do so. You remind me of a little bird I found some months ago fluttering along in the road with a broken wing. It pecked me several times when I picked it up, due to its great fear, and then——' He stopped abruptly and she stared at him, fascinated by the thought of this giant of a man bothering about something so small and insignificant as an injured bird.

'And then?' she asked quietly.

'Its heart simply stopped beating.' There was something in his eyes she couldn't read, something veiled behind the startling hypnotic gaze trained on her face. 'If it had just relaxed a little, trusted me a little, I would have been able to help it.'

She licked her lips nervously and then stopped abruptly as his eyes followed the gesture, lingering on the tremulous curve of her mouth.

'That is all I wish to do with this little bird.' He smiled very slowly but for the life of her she couldn't respond. 'Just help out. But——' he walked to the door and opened it quietly, turning with his hand on the brass knob to glance back at her again '—if you do not want to come to my home then you do not have to. It just seemed obvious, that is all. The doctor will be along shortly and I will return at lunchtime, when you can tell me what you have decided. If you choose to avail yourself of my hospitality you must be ready to leave then. Otherwise——' he shrugged Latin-style '—you may stay on here while you make other arrangements.' And then he had gone, the door shutting with a firm click only to open again a second later. 'One more thing—my sister lives with me in Marrakesh so you will not be entirely without a chaperon.' The heavy eyebrows quirked mockingly. 'Not that you will need one, of course.'

Alone again she stared at the closed door with a small frown wrinkling her brow. 'Not that you will need one.' She sank back against the pillows feeling both disgruntled and relieved. He obviously didn't find her in the least attractive, that much he had made crystal-clear. And that was good. Of course it was. She brushed an inoffensive crumb savagely off the sheet. She could just imagine his taste in women; voluptuous, sexy, possessing good bodies and the knowledge of how to use them. Big breasts, generous hips, pouting mouths... The mental description suddenly sparked the ghost of something in her mind, an image she couldn't drag out of the misty darkness to examine more closely before it had gone. She stared blindly across the small room, her face white with strain. Perhaps she had been more right than she knew when she asked if Gerard thought she was unbalanced; this certainly couldn't be normal. She groaned softly as she turned over on her side to await the appearance of the all-knowing doctor. Well, one thing was certain; there was no way, no way at all, she was leaving this place with Gerard Dumont, sister or no sister.

They left the clinic at precisely half-past three in the afternoon, and after the relative coolness of the air-conditioned building the white heat outside was overpowering.

'All right?' Gerard's eyes were tight on her face as they walked to his car, a low-slung sports model in jet black that looked as if it would bite if provoked.

'Fine.' She wasn't, of course. The heat was amazing but it was the dazzling brilliance of the blazing light that was causing problems, sending sharp little pinpricks of pain through her head as though it were being methodically stabbed with a keenly pointed blade. But even that wasn't the main reason for the trembling that seemed to have taken over her limbs and the palpitations that were causing a violent, irregular beating of her heart and a sick churning in her stomach. It was him. This virile, overwhelmingly masculine man at her side who dwarfed her not inconsiderable height by a good six inches and exuded an air of pure unadulterated sensual magnetism that was both dangerous and darkly attractive.

Why had she ever agreed to leave with him? she asked herself silently as she slid into the beautiful car just as her legs felt as though they wouldn't support her for another second. She hadn't meant to. But somehow...somehow he had swept all her objections aside with cool logic and a distant kind of friendliness that reassured even as she wondered if it were genuine. The call from his sister had helped too. She glanced at him now as he slid into the car at her side. 'Why did you ask Colette to phone me?' she asked tentatively. 'I mean——'

'I know what you mean,' he said mockingly as the sleek car growled into life. 'And you are right, partly...' He turned to eye her briefly, his face cynical and closed. 'You thought I had used her to promote what I wanted, is that it?' She stared at him without answering, wondering if it were too late to jump out of the car and run back to the relative protection of the impersonal clinic. 'Well, maybe I did, but it is for your own good, let me make that perfectly clear. This is a foreign country, or we'll assume it is a foreign country until we find out differently,' he added as she opened her mouth to make that very point, 'and one does not always play by the Marquis of Queensbery's rules here.' The tawny gaze was glittering now, reflecting the sun's brilliance as he held her wide grey eyes mesmerised. 'You are very definitely the bird with the broken wing at the moment, however much you dislike the analogy, and as such prey to all kinds of dangers. Do you know that in some quarters you would fetch a king's ransom?'

'What?' She couldn't believe she'd heard right for a moment.

'Make no mistake about it.' His mouth was harsh now as his gaze wandered over the red-brown hair and pale creamy skin. 'With your English looks and that air of untouched virginity, you would be snapped up within days.' He leant back in the seat as her mouth twisted in disbelief. 'You do not believe me? That alone tells me I was right. A babe among wolves...'

Was he going to sell her to some sheikh or white-slave trader? Was that it? She stared at him dumbly, unaware of the terror in her eyes. She had authorisation from the police to stay with him. They knew where to contact her. Lots of people did. Surely he wouldn't have organised all that if he intended——

'Colette exists.' His voice was very dry now as he read her thoughts. 'My home exists. I am a perfectly normal man who would not have slept particularly well at night if I had let you be cast adrift into an uncertain world. The telephone conversation with Colette was satisfactory?'

'Colette?' She pulled her thoughts together and moistened paper-dry lips carefully. 'Yes, of course.'

'You can spend some time talking with a female companion of your own age and perhaps something will be remembered, a spark that will unlock the door, yes?' He put a very large hand over hers resting on her knees, and she forced herself not to jerk away although his touch fired the alarm button. 'Now we have to drive to the small airfield where my plane is waiting. It will not take long.'

'Your plane?' She began to feel slightly hysterical. This wasn't happening to her, it couldn't be. She still wasn't quite sure how she came to be sitting in this prowling beast of a car with its master, anyway. As his hands moved to the leather-clad steering-wheel and he manoeuvred the powerful car out of the tiny hospital car park, she forced herself to think rationally, to get her emotions under control. She had made enquiries, independent enquiries, that morning with the police and the surprisingly sympathetic doctor, who had spent some considerable time with her trying to probe for something, anything, from her past, all to no avail.

She had discovered Gerard Dumont was an eminently respected businessman in Morocco, owning several businesses in Casablanca, Essaouira and Marrakesh involving the processing of fish and fruit, as well as his own fleet of freighters for goods to be sent overseas, and homes in each of the towns. He was enormously wealthy, a dignified and decorous citizen of the land his parents had moved to before he was born and altogether, according to her reports, a paragon of virtue. Except... Her eyes narrowed as she remembered the doctor's hesitation when she had asked if Gerard was married or involved with a particular woman.

'Not a particular woman, no...' The doctor had smiled carefully after a long moment of silence. 'But he is a young man in the prime of life; obviously there are stories . . .'

'Stories?' she had squeaked nervously, but the elderly man had not allowed himself to be drawn into a discussion about such an illustrious personage, parrying her questions adroitly until she had to give up gracefully. He had told her Gerard's parents had died many years before, that his sister was engaged to be married to a French Moroccan of impeccable breeding, and that if she accepted Gerard's invitation, which the doctor made clear he thought was an extremely generous and benevolent one, she would be treated with great respect and care as befitted the guest of such an important man. The phone call from Colette had clinched her indecision. Gerard's sister had sounded so bubbly and natural and genuinely concerned about her misfortune and anxious to help. It had all seemed cut and dried . . . until she had seen him again. Then all the doubts and fears returned with renewed vigour.

'You do not like me much, little one, do you?' It was a statement, not a question, and after one darting glance at the harsh profile she decided silence was definitely the best policy. There was nothing she could say, after all. She didn't like him; in fact everything about him grated on her like barbed wire even though she kept telling herself it was the height of ingratitude when he had been so kind. His height, the powerful masculine body, his arrogance and total domination of everything and everyone around him . . . It bothered her. Bothered her and frightened her and—— She shut off her thoughts abruptly. She didn't trust him. Not an inch. She didn't know why and probably there was no foundation for how she felt, but it was a fact.

She glanced again at his face and saw that the hard mouth was curved in a cynical, mocking smile. And that grated too.

'I will be interested to find out who you are, my sharp-clawed kitten,' he said softly after a few miles had passed in complete silence, the atmosphere tense and taut. 'I like honesty in people, men and women, and you are not short of that commodity.'

'You do?'

'I do.' She heard the thread of amusement in the dark seductive voice, and bit her lip tightly. 'I am clearly the lesser of two very real evils and it is a long time since I have been cast in such a role, especially by a woman.' The glittering gold eyes moved swiftly over her wary face before returning to the road. 'Especially such a beautiful woman.'

'You said you didn't find me attractive,' she retorted quickly in surprise before she had time to consider her words.

'I lied.' The deep voice was quite unrepentent.

As her stomach turned over in one flying leap she hunted for something to say, a casual remark that would defuse the sudden tension, but couldn't think of a thing, and as the miles continued to be eaten up by the beautiful car she forced herself to relax and concentrate on the changing scene outside the car window. And it was fascinating. Varied as Morocco was in its geography and climate, ranging from dry, gravelly plains extending for hundreds of miles and bleak shifting sand-dunes to rich tablelands in the Middle Atlas Mountains that furnished grazing for sheep and goats, the higher slopes covered in oak, cedar and pine and rich in ski resorts for the wealthy where rocky springs, lakes and ponds abounded as well as streams well stocked with trout, still nothing could be more varied than the spectrum of people who inhabited the land.

Every town and city had its Moroccan and European businessmen in traditional European dress side by side with Berbers and Arabs in flowing robes and wide, loose hoods, the women veiled and dressed in sober grey and black. And the transport... As Kit stared out of the window, the odd sumptuous car rode alongside decrepit taxis, wicked-eyed camels, horses, donkeys, bikes and every other mode of transport known to man. The buildings were piercingly white, Moorish architecture showing its grace and beauty in sunlit streets lined with orange trees... She sank back against the upholstered seat with a small sigh, her senses sated. She couldn't live here; she must be on holiday—it was all too new and exciting. Holiday? But she'd left because of an argument, a ring...? She glanced down at her ringless hands and her brow wrinkled and that sick feeling of dread reared its head, before both the image and emotion faded as quickly as they had come.

'What is it?' She suddenly realised Gerard had been talking to her and she hadn't heard a word, and now saw they had left the confines of the town and were out on the boundary road. 'You have remembered something?'

'Not really.' She rubbed a damp hand over her brow as she shut her eyes for a brief moment. 'It was gone before I could make sense of it. I'm sorry, what did you say?'

'I wondered if you had ever seen goats climbing trees before,' he said drily. 'Over there, look.' As he brought the car to a standstill she peered where he was pointing, and saw a host of argan trees, their low spreading limbs covered with green leaves and small fruits that looked like olives, and then as her eyes rose upwards she was amazed to see several goats high in the branches nibbling away at the leaves and fruit, one or two of the sure-footed little creatures having ventured far out on the branches as they stretched for the tenderest morsels.

'They really are goats!' she breathed in surprise, her eyes stretched wide.

Gerard laughed softly, delighted with her astonishment. 'These trees are not found anywhere else in the world,' he said quietly as he started the engine again after several long minutes, 'and the goats adore the fruit. The seeds you see on the ground there——' he pointed to the mass of fruit seeds scattered under the trees '—are gathered up and washed and cracked and from the inner nut is drawn a fragrant oil used for cooking. Not that the goats care about that, of course.' He eyed her lazily before drawing on to the dusty road again.

The little incident had broken the tension for a time, but the very nearness of that big masculine body in the close confines of the car made her as jumpy as a cricket. Did he really find her attractive? she asked herself silently as the car purred on. That last look he'd given her, there had been something in the slumberous depths that had caused her lower stomach to tighten in immediate response, and she had hated herself for it, hated herself without understanding the reason why. But then there was nothing she *did* understand at the moment anyway, she told herself flatly. She was a mess.

They reached the small airfield where Gerard's private plane was kept amid a cloud of dust, and it wasn't until she was airborne, with Gerard at the controls, that she thought to ask about the location of Marrakesh. Everything had seemed so unreal, so nebulous, since she had woken up in the hospital that she still was finding it hard to convince herself that she wasn't in the grip of a dream . . . or a nightmare.

'Marrakesh?' Gerard's deep voice was thoughtful. 'Let me see. Well, it is the most African city of Morocco, at the foothills of the High Atlas Mountains due south of Casablanca. The region is dry but water has been piped down from the mountains into reservoirs, so a bath will be no problem.' He eyed her fleetingly, his expression searching and she flushed hotly. It was just as if he had undressed her.

'We have the normal old and new side by side,' he continued, after the twist of his mouth informed her he knew exactly what she was thinking. 'Modern agriculture, training schools and various industries as well as a camel market every Thursday that dates back into ancient history, and a fair in the great square of Djemaa-el-Fna that involves snake charmers, magicians, jugglers, acrobats and even the odd medicine man demonstrating miraculous cures in their bottles. I'll show you around once you are settled in; there are some wonderful medieval palaces and monuments——'

'No, there's no need for that.' She had interrupted him so abruptly that she hastened to qualify her refusal. 'I mean, I don't want to inconvenience you at all, Mr Dumont, you've been very kind and I'll be gone within a day or so——'

'Gerard.' Suddenly the handsome face was intimidatingly cold and harsh, the profile flinty. 'And please do not try to spare my feelings. Colette will do just as well as your guide.'

'I didn't mean——'

He interrupted her again, his voice dry. 'I know exactly what you meant; you neither like or trust me so let us leave it at that. I hope you will be reassured when you reach my home but, as you so graciously pointed out, it will be a matter of days until this matter resolves itself so your opinion of me is really of no importance to either of us.'

She deserved it. She knew she deserved it but nevertheless the icy autocratic tone made her see red. 'Look, I'm sorry,' she said tightly, her voice tense. 'If it's any consolation *I* don't understand why I'm acting like this, but when all's said and done I didn't ask to come with you, did I? Why did you insist——?'

'I am damned if I know,' he bit back angrily.

'Well, just turn the plane round and take me back to Casablanca——' she began furiously, only to stop abruptly as she realised the import of what she had just said. Casablanca? Why had she said Casablanca? The accident had happened on the streets of Essaouira, hadn't it?

'Casablanca,' Gerard repeated thoughtfully at her side, obviously catching the importance of her words too. 'I think we should perhaps ask the police to direct their enquiries more specifically in that city, yes?'

'I don't know.' She shook her head wearily, the spurt of rage dying as quickly as it had flared into life as she stared down at the white cotton trousers and neat coffee-coloured blouse that had been pressed and cleaned by the cheerful little nurse at the nursing home. Some time, in another life, she had actually chosen these things, walked into a shop and made the purchases of her own accord. *How could she not remember*?

'I will take care of it.' He spared her a quick glance, his face expressionless. 'And I do not intend to eat you alive, my thorny rose, but for the sake of my sanity, if not yours, could you please refrain from the cat-on-a-hot-tin-roof syndrome? My ego is beginning to feel a little fragile.'

'I'm sorry.' She stared down at her hands miserably.

'So you said.' The deep rich voice was cynically mocking again and immediately the guilt she had been feeling was replaced by hot anger. A fragile ego? Him? Not in a million years.

The fierce heat of the day was dying when they reached the huge strip of ground on the outskirts of Marrakesh which formed part of Gerard's estate. As he taxied the light plane into the hangar she saw a beautiful white Ferrari parked some distance away, its tinted windows and enormous side grilles proclaiming it a Testarossa. 'Your car?' She gestured resignedly towards the magnificent vehicle.

'My car,' he agreed gravely, his voice bland. 'Do you like it?'

'It's very nice.'

She heard a snort at her side and turned to see that he was surveying her with a dark frown, his eyes narrowed. 'Don't tell me,' he drawled slowly, the relaxed tone belying the sharpness in his eyes, 'for some reason you disapprove of the car.' It was a statement, not a question. 'Why do I get the feeling that if anyone else had owned it you would have given it the appreciation such functional beauty deserves?'

'I said it was very nice,' she protested carefully, aware of the truth in his words, 'but a car is just a car, isn't it? A grown-up child's toy?'

'A toy?' He shut his eyes briefly after killing the engine of the plane, and then opened them slowly, the narrowed slits gleaming gold. 'There is a six-year waiting list for this toy, as it happens.'

She hadn't noticed the middle-aged Arab standing to one side of the hangar but now, as Gerard jumped down from the plane and reached up to assist her, she saw the hangar doors being closed before the small man hurried across to them.

'Assad...' The two exchanged greetings and then Gerard turned to her, his face relaxed and smiling now. 'This is my great friend and man of all trades, Assad. You would not have noticed him at the time, but as chance would have it he was just entering my office building when you were attacked and saw it all,' Gerard continued quietly, 'not that it proved much help in the event. He speaks French, Spanish and Arabic but little English incidentally. None of my house staff does, unfortunately.'

'Oh.' She stared at them both feeling completely out of her depth, and as she turned away to glance again at the Ferrari she missed the softening of Gerard's mouth that indicated he was aware of just how she felt.

'The house is just a few hundred yards away but I asked Assad to bring the car in case you were tired. Shall we?' He indicated the car with a wave of his hand. 'Assad will see to the plane and follow shortly.'

She found, as she walked to the car, that she *was* tired, a deep exhaustion taking hold of her body and mind that made even the smallest response a superhuman effort. As Gerard held open the door she climbed slowly into the luxurious interior, her head pounding. 'Thank you.' She raised dull eyes to his and saw him frown slightly before he left to walk round the bonnet and slide in beside her.

'You need a warm bath and plenty of sleep,' he said levelly as he nosed the car out of the hangar and along a dry dust road towards a mass of trees in the distance. 'Both of which will prove no problem at Del Mahari. My home,' he added at her glance of enquiry.

'Del Mahari?' She let the foreign name slide over her lips. 'That sounds nice.'

'It means "Racing Camel",' he said expressionlessly, although she was sure there was a thread of amusement colouring the deep voice. 'My father enjoyed the sport, although I prefer to keep horses rather than camels. I find the latter singly unattractive creatures and more than a little bad-tempered, although that trait is not confined to camels, of course,' he added smoothly as he kept his eyes fixed ahead. She glanced at him warily, knowing it was a gibe at her but unable to respond to such an indirect insult. 'At the moment I have several beautifully trained horses of great speed and stamina who have mingled Arab and Berber strains in their blood line. Do you ride?'

The question was casual and she answered before she considered, the reply instinctive. 'Oh, yes, I love...' Her voice trailed away for a second before she recovered. 'Yes, I know I ride,' she said more firmly. 'I don't know how I know but I do.'

'Good.' They had reached the trees now which she saw were fruit trees, mainly orange, surrounding the outside of a rosy pink extremely high wall in which two huge iron gates were set standing open ready for the Ferrari to pass through, but Gerard stopped the car just before the gates and cut the engine slowly, turning to her and touching her face gently with one finger as he turned her face to his. 'Welcome to my home, little kitten,' he said softly, seconds before his warm, hard mouth captured hers.

CHAPTER THREE

IF SOMEONE had poured boiling water over her head Kit could not have reacted more violently. For a split-second, just an infinitesimal moment of time, she had frozen as his firm sensual mouth had captured hers, the smell and feel of him all-encompassing, and then she jerked away so savagely that her head ricocheted off the car window with a resounding bang that caused the air to vibrate.

'What on earth?' Gerard looked as shocked as she felt as he surveyed her beneath dark frowning brows. 'I was only kissing you, girl; what the hell did you think I intended?'

'I...' Her voice trailed away as she stared at him wide-eyed in the shadowed dusk, aware of the sweet odour of flowering jasmine being borne on the soft warm night air. 'I don't know, I'm sorry...' As her voice petered out again she took a deep breath as she tried to compose herself. 'But I didn't expect you to do that. I'm here as your guest, aren't I? I thought——'

'It was a kiss of welcome,' he ground out tightly. 'Nothing more, nothing less.' His eyes raked her face angrily.

'I'm sorry.' There didn't seem anything else to say and she was suddenly aware that she had made a terrible fool of herself.

'Then let us try it again?' It was the last thing she had expected him to say, and she stared at him with wide dove-grey eyes, the smudge of freckles across her nose standing out in sharp contrast to the pale creamy skin surrounding them. 'A kiss, nothing more,' he reassured softly as he leant forward again, his eyes liquid gold in the dim light. 'I won't hurt you.'

As he lightly stroked her sealed lips with his hard, sensual mouth she began to feel herself tremble, the sensations the gentle caress was producing warm and sweet to her shattered senses, and as he felt her helpless reaction the kiss deepened, his tongue invading the sanctuary of her mouth as she opened her lips to gasp at the heat spreading through her body. A kiss? This was a kiss? If she had ever been kissed like this before she would have remembered, she knew it.

One of his arms slid round her seat, his hand moving to the small of her back to urge her more intimately against his big frame, but he made no move to touch her beyond that, although she could feel the pounding of his heart against the solid wall of his chest. His lips left hers for a moment to wander languorously over her closed eyelids, her ears, her throat, before returning to her half-open mouth to plunder the soft interior yet again. And then he raised his head as he moved back into his own seat, and the departure was almost like a betrayal.

'As I said, welcome to my home,' he said softly as she opened dazed eyes to focus on the tawny brown gaze. 'I hope you will be happy here.'

He had started the engine before she could reply, and as they drove through the massive gates into the lush garden beyond she tried desperately to control the trembling that had taken hold of her limbs. This was a man she didn't like, didn't trust and barely knew, and she could react like that to his touch? What on earth was she? She didn't dare look at the big dark figure next to her, trying to focus her eyes and her thoughts on her surroundings and nothing else.

They appeared to be moving through an orchard, the wide winding drive snaking past olive, orange, almond and fig trees, and then the house was there in front of her, a magnificent white structure in traditional Moroccan design with delicate ornamentation and beautifully carved arches that looked as though they were covered in lace, so fine and intricate were the traceries on them.

Gerard drew the car to a halt in front of the massive arched front door studded in brass, which was immediately opened from within to reveal a small, slender woman of thirty or so who moved out on to the top step, her brown face wreathed in smiles and her body swathed in the Moroccan jellaba, a long loose robe of cotton. 'This is Assad's wife, Amina,' Gerard whispered quietly as he raised his hand in greeting. 'Assad's brother, Abou, also works here with his wife Halima and their family. Unfortunately Assad and Amina have no children, which has been a source of great grief to them, although Assad has resisted the temptation to take a second wife, which is quite permissable for him under Moslem law, especially if his first wife is barren.'

'Who says it's her that's at fault?' Kit asked quietly, annoyed at the inference. 'Couldn't it be Assad?'

'Quite possibly,' Gerard said drily by her side as he moved to open his door. 'But if you value your well-being do not even breathe such heresy within Assad's hearing.' He walked lazily round the car to open her door, helping her out of the low vehicle with a hand on the crook of her elbow. 'Moroccan men are extremely proud of their virility.'

'Not just Moroccan men,' she whispered back tightly. 'I think your whole sex can be incredibly unfair in this sort of situation. Couldn't you do something about it, help them in some way?'

'Not until Assad saw fit to mention the matter to me,' Gerard said coolly. 'It would be considered the height of impropriety for anyone other than he to raise such a delicate matter.'

'I think you men can be the most stupid creatures on the earth,' she murmured out of the side of her mouth as they began to walk up the gleaming stone steps towards Amina.

'That is what you think, is it?' The deep voice held a satirical, mocking note that made her want to kick him, hard. 'It will be a brave man indeed that takes you in hand, little kitten, but the rewards could be . . . interesting.'

Amina greeted them very prettily, although Kit didn't understand a word the diminutive Moroccan woman said, but the warmth in her brown face and sparkling eyes was welcome enough.

Gerard took her arm again as they passed through the front door and she found herself immediately descending two flights of large wide marble steps to pass out through another arch into a beautifully cool courtyard, shaded by banana trees, bougainvillaea vines and other flowering tropical plants flourishing in riotous colour and profusion amid the murmur of several whispering fountains.

'How gorgeous, how absolutely gorgeous.' She turned to him impulsively to find he was watching her with narrowed gold eyes, his face expressionless. 'What a beautiful home you have, Gerard.'

'I am most fortunate,' he agreed quietly after a long heart-stopping moment when his gaze remained fixed on her half-open mouth. 'I have apartments in Essaouira and Casablanca, which were a practical investment due to the amount of time I spend in the towns overseeing my businesses there, but this is the only place I consider home. Come, I will show you all of it and then we will have some refreshments that Amina has prepared before you retire.'

The rest of the winding, spreading house stretched and unfurled before her as she wandered round the high, gracious rooms on Gerard's arm. Several rooms had sofas and chaises-longues with low tables, desks and shelves fashioned beautifully in fine wood and inlaid with thin pieces of gold and silver and wood of a different hue. Expensive books bound in Moroccan leather and gold leaf lined several walls, ornamented guns and daggers, trays of hammered brass and copper and finely worked marble figurines were scattered tastefully throughout the house.

On the lower level the floors were covered by fine Persian carpets and on the first level, where the bedrooms stretched almost into infinity each with its own *en suite* bathroom, the floors were of the finest polished wood with beautifully designed rugs scattered in each room.

By the time they returned to the large courtyard the night sky was alive with tiny glittering stars and the sweet, heavy perfume of flowering jasmine and magnolia hung rich and intoxicating in the still warm air. Amina was waiting for them with a taller, slightly older woman, whom Gerard introduced as Halima, Amina's sister-in-law. Like Amina she had a sweet, gentle face and her manner was graceful. Kit felt the two got on well in spite of the difficulty that Amina's lack of a family would undoubtedly cause between the two couples.

'Eat a little; it will please them,' Gerard said quietly as he noticed her somewhat bemused glance at the low wide table filled with seemingly hundreds of dishes of different food, as well as bowls of ripe apricots, cherries, pears, plums, figs and grapes. She felt so exhausted now that she was working on automatic, eating a little fruit and one heavily spiced sweet pastry and drinking several tiny glasses of the very sweet green tea flavoured with mint that the Moroccans rated so highly, before leaning back in her chair and trying to force her eyelids not to close.

Nevertheless she must have fallen asleep, because the next thing she became aware of was being cradled in a pair of very strong masculine arms as she was carried upstairs. 'Gerard?' She opened dazed eyes to see his dark tanned face an inch or two from hers. 'I'm sorry, did I fall asleep? I can walk——'

'Be quiet.' His voice was soft and low. 'In two minutes you will be tucked up in bed and able to sleep as long as you like.'

If it was meant to reassure, it didn't, as she suddenly became aware of his hard body next to hers as he moved. The smell and feel of his alien maleness encompassed her, his almost menacing strength and power as he carried her up the stairs causing a wild, fluttering panic in her chest. Did he think *he* was going to tuck her into bed? she thought silently with a faint touch of hysteria, and *whose* bed—his?

'Colette went shopping for you this afternoon,' he continued steadily as they reached the landing and continued down the wide corridor to an open door halfway down. 'Unfortunately she had a dinner engagement with her future in-laws this evening and was unable to welcome you personally, but she will see you tomorrow.'

'Thank you...' She felt ridiculously vulnerable as he entered the room, a vision of the East in flowing wall drapes, large sunken bed and exquisitely delicate carved furniture.

He set her down carefully on a long low couch to one side of the bed and straightened to survey her with narrowed eyes. 'Can you manage without help?' he asked expressionlessly.

'Yes, of course,' she answered hastily, too hastily, and as her hand went protectively to the top button of her blouse she saw his mouth tighten.

'I wasn't going to suggest that I undress you,' he said with a cool smoothness that told her she had annoyed him. 'Amina would be only too pleased to help you.'

'I don't need anyone,' she answered quickly, her eyes flickering as he crossed his muscled arms over his broad chest, his face reflective.

'We all need someone.' He had deliberately taken her words out of context and they both knew it. 'You are not an island or a ship that sails alone over the sea of life——'

'I'm not a boarding vessel either.' She hadn't meant to say it, the words had just popped out of their own volition, but once said there was no taking them back and she stared at him aghast for a second as she waited to see his reaction.

'I am very tempted to do one of two things,' he said thoughtfully after a long silent moment when his eyes had taken on the consistency of splintered ice. 'One, in spite of your recent accident, is to take you over my knee and spank the hell out of that cute behind in the hope that the short, sharp shock treatment might knock some sense into the top part of your anatomy. The other...' He paused, his face hard. 'The other is to show you exactly what it would mean if I took you into my arms and decided to make real love to you.'

'You dare, you just dare,' she murmured desperately, terrified he would follow one of the threats through. 'You told me I was coming here as your guest, that you just regarded me as a fellow human being in need of help——'

'I told you before, I lied,' he said silkily, 'or at least it was partly a lie. You *are* here as my guest and you *are* a human being who needs help. You are also a very lovely and desirable young woman—surely it is not untoward of me to notice this?'

'There's noticing and noticing,' she said weakly.

'You mean I should not want you in my bed?' he asked with deceptive mildness. 'I am a normal thirty-five-year-old man, in case you had not noticed.' Oh, she'd noticed all right, she thought shakily—boy, had she noticed! 'Now while I certainly have never been promiscuous, neither have I been celibate since my youth.' He eyed her lazily. 'And no doubt, if you could remember, we would find that this air of innocence which I have to admit is so attractive is not a factual physical reality either.'

'Would we indeed?' she asked flatly as her pulse leapt. 'Well, I'll let you know when I know, shall I?' She was aiming at heavy sarcasm but he merely nodded his head sagely, his expression remote.

'If you like.'

'No, I don't actually.' She swung round on the couch and brought her feet to the floor, her knees tightly together and her hands in her lap. 'I don't like any of this conversation——'

'Why?' He interrupted her immediately, his eyes darkening. 'What has happened, that you cannot relate to a man except with hostility and distrust? You are young, lovely——'

'Look, please stop saying I'm lovely,' she said sharply. 'I might have lost my memory temporarily but I'm not stupid and I *have* looked in the mirror since I had that bang on the head. I'm passable, that's all, and you know it.'

'Passable?' His voice was soft now and very deep, and a trembling little shiver snaked down her spine although he hadn't moved an inch. 'Hair the colour and texture of red-brown silk, creamy skin that is as clear as fresh water, a mouth generous enough to drive a man wild, eyes like warm dusk——'

'Stop it.' The heat in her lower stomach forced the exclamation out of her mouth. 'Please, I don't want this.' She wasn't aware of the tortured pleading in her wide eyes or the tremulous curve of her mouth as she fought for control, but to the tall man watching her so closely, the body language said it all. Someone had hurt her, hurt her very badly, and in that moment he could cheerfully have committed murder if the man were there in front of him. His own body stirred fiercely, reminding him of the desire that had been paramount since almost the first moment of seeing her, and again he asked himself why.

It was true that she wasn't outrageously beautiful in the traditional sense: the tall slender body was as slim as a young boy's, her breasts small and firm against the material of the blouse she wore. Not the type he usually admired at all. And her hair, cut so short that it was almost severe, the lack of make-up, of any normal female adornment... No. To all intents and purposes she shouldn't move him at all and yet—— And yet she did.

'Go to sleep now.' He turned on his heel abruptly, his face dark and closed, and strode towards the open door, pausing to turn on the threshold, his eyes veiled. 'And you can sleep in peace, no one will disturb you here. You understand?'

'Yes.' She stared back at him, her face pale against the rich reds and golds in which the room was decorated. 'I understand.'

And amazingly, in spite of all the doubts and fears and the heavy darkness that seemed to permeate even her sleep, she drifted into a thick deep slumber as soon as she settled herself among the luxurious silk sheets and tumbled pillows of the enormous sunken bed, sleeping through the night and far, far into the next day until Amina entered the shaded room later the following afternoon.

'Mademoiselle sleepy? Verrry sleepy?' Amina's heavily accented voice was soft and melodious as Kit opened vague dazed eyes as the small woman drew the fine drapes from the open window to reveal the shimmering blueness of the late afternoon sky. 'Now feast? Good, eh?'

'I'm sorry...' Kit was just staring at her non-plussed when a warm female chuckle from the open doorway brought her head swinging round.

'She wants you to eat something.' The small, finely boned woman standing on the threshold indicated the tray Amina had just picked up from a low table. 'Dinner won't be until much later. I'm Colette, by the way.'

So saying, Gerard's sister strode across the room and plumped down at the side of the bed on a thick Persian rug so that she was directly on an eyeline with Kit, who had struggled into a sitting position amid the rumpled sheets. 'That nightie all right? I didn't know what your taste would be, not having met you.' She grinned, a warm natural grin that showed lots of small white teeth.

'It's lovely.' Kit glanced down vacantly at the pale green lace. 'It was very good of you to go to so much trouble.'

'No trouble,' Colette said cheerily. 'Orders from the boss.' She grinned again and Kit couldn't help smiling back, thinking as she did so how different Colette was from her huge handsome brother. No more than five feet two, small and delicately made, she exuded an air of petite feminine attractiveness that went well with the tiny heart-shaped face, huge green eyes and mass of burnished copper hair. There was no trace of an accent in her voice either, Kit thought in surprise. Really, brother and sister couldn't be more different. 'How do you feel?' Colette eyed her consideringly.

'Much better for that sleep,' Kit answered quickly. 'It's very nice to meet you.'

'Nice to meet you,' Colette returned immediately, 'although you aren't at all what I imagined you to be.'

'No?' Kit found herself grinning unexpectedly at the note of surprise in the other girl's voice. 'You aren't what I thought either. You're not at all like your brother, are you?'

'Thank goodness!' Colette wrinkled a pert nose. 'I'll take that as a compliment! What woman wants to be six feet four and built like Tarzan anyway? Actually...' She paused for a second. 'We're half-brother and -sister. Gerard's mother died when he was very small and Dad met my mother three years later. She was an American,' she added as she took the tray for Amina who left them with a bob of her head, 'and constantly homesick. She used to spend half her time here with Dad, whom she loved like crazy, and half in America with her tribe of relations. I used to go with her of course, but Gerard never did. He preferred to stay at Del Mahari with Dad. It sounds like a weird kind of arrangement, I know, but it suited all of us. I honestly can't remember any of the family having a cross word when Mum and Dad were still alive.'

Kit wanted to reply to the casual confidence, she really did, but as Colette had finished speaking something had pierced her heart with such intensity that it was a physical pain. There was something she had to remember, something vital, but even as she sought for it it had vanished as Colette's voice broke into her mind again, urgent this time.

'Are you all right? You look——'

'She looks as though she could do without your chatter for a time.'

As both girls turned as one towards the deep voice, Kit felt her heart stop for a stunned moment and then rush on at a pace that took her breath away. Gerard was standing in the doorway, his golden-brown hair with its vibrant tawny sheen blazing in a shaft of sunlight that turned the narrowed eyes into slits of gold, and the big, powerful body clothed in loose cotton trousers and a thin, long-sleeved robe caught at the waist with a belt of embroidered material. The front of the tunic was slashed to the waist in a wide V, showing the hard-muscled chest densely covered by dark, curling body hair, and as Kit watched him move into the room the sensual pull of the man was so strong she could taste it. The Arab clothes seemed made for him, the European façade falling away as though by magic.

'You slept well?' The charming accent tugged at her nerves and it was some seconds before she could speak.

'Very well, thank you.' His feet were bare, she noticed dazedly as he came to stand by the side of the sunken bed before crouching down by her side with a slight smile.

'Good. And Colette's chatter has not tired you?'

'I've only been in here a couple of minutes,' his sister protested indignantly, with a scathing glance at her brother which the dark tanned face ignored completely.

'And now you are going to leave so our guest can eat her meal in peace.' The deep voice was silky smooth but neither of the two women missed the thread of steel underneath, and Kit was surprised to see Colette capitulate immediately, her only objection a slight grimace, and even more surprised at the flood of hot anger that the little by-play brought surging forth in *her* chest. He really was the most arrogant, high-handed——

'Don't frown.' As Colette left the room with a little wave of her hand and a cheerful smile she saw Gerard's eyes were tight on her face and tried to smooth out her expression quickly. 'And eat your meal; it is only a little cold meat and salad with a glass of wine.'

'You drink alcohol?' she asked slowly. 'But I thought——'

'I am French, not Moroccan,' he answered quietly, 'and not of the Moslem religion. I am in the fortunate position of being able to choose what suits me best out of two cultures—an enviable arrangement, do you not agree?' He was talking lightly, his attitude relaxed and easy, but for the life of her Kit couldn't respond. His nearness had tied her stomach into a giant knot and never had she been more acutely aware of her own body. The flimsy nightie that Colette had chosen left nothing to the imagination, and although the second she had heard his voice she had pulled one of the silk sheets high to her chin, she still felt helplessly exposed and curiously threatened. In his Western clothes he had been formidable but here, in his own surroundings and wearing what obviously suited him best, he had all the reassuring attributes of a prowling lion. She couldn't stay here, she really couldn't, and she should never have come...

'Dinner is at eight.' As he straightened she caught a whiff of something heady and again her heart pounded as though it were going to jump out of her body. Stop it, *stop it*. She shut her eyes tight for a second, furious with her weakness at what was only, after all, a chemical reaction to his overpowering maleness. He probably dressed like that on purpose, she thought balefully, as she watched him stride out of the room after a brief nod at her closed face, but no... Even as the thought took form she knew it was unfair. He was himself, that was all. And it was more than enough.

It took quite some time to force the food past the tension in her chest but she managed it at last, sipping the glass of light sparkling wine as she lay back against the rich silk pillows. What a room! She glanced round the exotic Eastern-style boudoir with something akin to wonder before padding across to the *en-suite* bathroom, with a swift nervous glance at the closed bedroom door before she ventured from the protection of the silk sheets.

After a long, cool shower she washed her hair under the flowing water before wrapping a thick bath-sheet tightly round her naked form and peering out into the bedroom beyond. What about clothes? Suddenly the practicalities of the situation she was in overwhelmed her. And make-up, creams, shoes...

The bathroom cabinet revealed a vast array of lotions and cosmetics as well as the more mundane essentials like toothpaste, tooth-brushes, all still in their packaging. Had Colette bought all this for her? She hoped not, she thought nervously as she made her way to the massive walk-in wardrobe at one end of the vast bedroom. This was embarrassing enough as it was. The wardrobe disclosed hanger upon hanger of European and Eastern clothes all roughly her size, with a large drawer of underwear, all lace and froth, at one side and several different pairs of shoes in sizes ranging from five to eight. She looked down at her slender feet thoughtfully. She didn't even know what size shoes she took, but she thought it was six. It was. The first pair of flat leather slip-ons she tried on fitted her perfectly.

By the time a huge gong rang through the house at exactly ten to eight, frightening the life out of her, she was dressed and ready to go downstairs and at least looking, if not feeling, in control. She had chosen an informal black dinner suit in thin silk, the large baggy trousers and thigh-length short-sleeved blouse a compromise between East and West, and apart from the vague thread of gold that featured intermittently in the material wore no other adornment, not even a trace of mascara. If anyone had told her she was trying to efface herself, to hide behind the severe colour, she would have denied it hotly and believed what she said.

Colette knocked on her door a moment after the last vibrations of the gong had died, taking her arm in a friendly hug as they walked down the massive curving stairs to the floor below. And Gerard was waiting.

She glanced at him nervously as he stood up, his big body uncoiling with sensuous grace from the low cushioned divan at one side of the huge hall, and as he walked towards them, the loose robes swirling about his hard muscled frame and his eyes narrowed and cool, she felt an immediate, and not unpleasant, rush of femininity in answer to his silent, powerful masculinity.

'Do not be nervous, it is just the three of us for dinner,' he said softly as he reached her side and, although it was meant as comfort, it did nothing to soothe her jangling nerves. She would have given the world to be oblivious to the sensations the big body clothed in sumptuous Arab raiment called forth from her own, but every muscle and sinew was alive and kicking. 'Have you eaten Moroccan style before?' he asked her quietly as he led the women into the dining-room, an arm round each of their waists.

'I don't think so.' She was concentrating very hard on putting one foot in front of the other and ignoring the heat from his casual hand on her skin.

'I find it more comfortable and conducive to conversation than the European way,' Gerard said lightly as he indicated one of the exquisitely embroidered sofas scattered around an enormous low table with the flick of a brown wrist. 'I hope you have no objection to eating with your fingers?' He raised an amused eyebrow at her surprise. 'One uses the right hand, incidentally, which is washed by Amina before the meal begins and again afterwards; she would be most shocked if you used the left.'

'Why?' Kit asked carefully as she seated herself as gracefully as she could on one of the upholstered sofas.

'The left is used for more mundane duties,' Gerard said blandly. 'In my father's time a thief was sometimes sentenced to have his right hand cut off which, besides branding him for life, kept him from ever again eating with other people and dipping into the communal dish. A cruel but most effective punishment.'

She eyed him from under her lashes. 'You aren't saying you approve of such barbarity?' she asked with horrified revulsion.

'Of course Gerard wouldn't approve,' Colette said easily as she flung herself down at her brother's side. 'He's a real old softie under that hard exterior.'

The dark eyebrows rose a fraction, but beyond that enigmatic recognition Gerard made no comment on Colette's statement which he obviously held in derisive disdain.

As Halima began bringing dish after dish to the large low table, Amina appeared with towels and a huge pottery basin, returning a moment later with a large receptacle similar to a kettle. As Kit held her right hand above the basin as Amina indicated, the small Moroccan woman poured a stream of soft, delicately scented water over it. 'It smells like roses,' Kit exclaimed in surprise to Gerard, who was watching her through slitted gold eyes, his expression unreadable.

'It is.' He smiled lazily. 'At the edge of the desert acres of rose bushes grow in fields of oases that stretch for nearly a hundred miles. When the roses bloom their petals are gathered in large baskets and carried off to a still to be boiled in water. In the still, the vapour that boils off is condensed into an oil called attar of roses, which is prized here for perfuming the ceremonial water. It pleases you?'

'Yes, of course.' She smiled nervously. There was a brooding intensity to the dark face that was quite unnerving. 'It's a lovely idea.'

'An ancient ritual,' he corrected gently, 'one of many that is most charming. I am not quite the savage you imagine.'

'I don't——'

But her protest was interrupted by Colette, who, quite oblivious to the undercurrents swirling about her, giggled light-heartedly at what she considered her brother's joke. 'You'll get used to him in time,' she laughed cheerfully, her small attractive face alight. 'Gerard, of all people, a savage!' She giggled again. 'I've never known anyone who knows as much about so many diverse topics as he does.'

'Ah, but that is head knowledge, Colette,' Gerard interrupted her coolly as Amina washed his hand, his gaze never leaving Kit's tight face for a moment. 'Nothing whatsoever to do with the inner man. We all have an element of the untamed lurking within, the beast that layers of civilisation cannot quite subdue. Is that not right, my English kitten?'

'You seem to know a lot about it,' she answered stiffly, 'and who am I to argue with someone who knows so much about everything?'

He opened his mouth to reply at the same moment as the telephone rang on a small table behind him. '*Là*.' He shook his head as Halima reached for it and picked up the receiver himself, listening intently for a few minutes before communicating in rapid Arabic with the person at the other end.

His face was closed and hard when he replaced the receiver at last, his eyes hooded and expressionless as they glanced across at Kit sitting quietly watching him. 'Who are you?' he said at last, echoing her words with a cold smile. 'It would seem you are a Miss Samantha Kittyn of London, England.' His gaze became piercing on her face, noting every flicker of expression. 'Or at least that is what the police have been told by your fiancé, a certain David Shore.'

CHAPTER FOUR

'WELL?' Gerard continued to hold Kit's eyes in a compelling stare. 'Does this information, as you say, ring any bells?'

'No.' She shook her head slowly, her face blank. 'Nothing at all.' *She was engaged? Engaged to be married*?

'I see.' She could have been imagining it, but just for a second she could have sworn it was relief mingled with satisfaction she saw mirrored in the glittering eyes. 'Perhaps this David is not the sort of man who makes a lasting impression?' The words were said so softly, with such a lack of expression, that for a moment the biting insult contained in the smooth voice didn't register, and by the time it did he had moved on detailing the essence of his conversation with the police inspector.

'After I telephoned the inspector in charge of your case today, the police concentrated their enquiries in Casablanca and it would seem almost immediately a report came to light. The Sabratha hotel were concerned this morning when one of their lone women guests, an Englishwoman, did not return as indicated the night before, and even more worried when the car she had hired was found in Essaouira by an enthusiastic police officer, to all appearances abandoned. When the police checked your papers, which were fortunately in the hotel safe, all became clear. They rang the address in England and spoke to your flatmate and also her brother, the said David.' The light brown eyes hardened. 'It would appear he wishes to speak with you as soon as this is possible.'

'Oh.' The effort it took to pull her gaze from his was disturbing, *he* was disturbing, this whole crazy drama was disturbing and she was right bang-smack in the middle of it.

'However, Amina and Halima are waiting for the meal to begin, so perhaps you could delay the call for a short time?' he asked silkily, although she knew, without questioning how, that he had no intention of encouraging her to phone David that night. Would he physically stop her? She glanced at the tall, lean body clothed in the flowing robes and, as her gaze travelled upwards, met light stony eyes that were as hard as nails. Perhaps, yes, perhaps, but it didn't matter anyway; she had no intention of telephoning a stranger in England and hearing goodness knew what until she had had time to collect her thoughts and decide what to ask.

At her acquiescent nod his eyes narrowed a little as though he were trying to gauge what was going on in her mind, but then he raised an authoritative hand to the two Moroccan women and the meal commenced.

As Amina and Halima placed in front of them a huge dish of roast lamb surrounded by several plates of small round loaves of delicious nutty

Arab bread, Gerard spoke quietly, his voice warm and relaxed now as he assumed the role of host again. 'It is customary to eat with the thumb and first two fingers of your right hand,' he said softly as he indicated for Colette to show her how, 'and as this is merely the first course of several, do not think you have to clear the dish.' He smiled slowly and, as before, her heart pounded at the difference it made to his autocratic, somewhat cold classical features. 'Amina and Halima will expect you to have a little of each course; they are delighted to have a guest that they can impress. The meat is so tender it will come away easily in the hand and it customary to have no plates unless you would like one?'

'No, no, this is fine,' she said hastily as she followed Colette's example and reached for a succulent piece of meat, finding the aroma irresistible. 'It's gorgeous.' She licked her greasy fingers appreciatively as she reached across for more, suddenly finding she was ravenously hungry.

When Amina arrived with the next course Kit's eyes turned automatically to Gerard and, as before, his gaze was trained on her face. 'This is a *pastilla*,' he said quietly, 'and Amina has spent many hours preparing it in your honour, so as you eat express your admiration. It consists of wafer-thin layers of flaky pastry filled with meat, almonds, hard boiled eggs, herbs and spices and will be very hot inside, so be careful.'

She nodded a dutiful response even as her heart began to thud violently in her chest. He looked so...foreign in the long loose robes of jade-green and black that clothed the big masculine body so carelessly, foreign and devastatingly, vitally male. Like a scene from the *Arabian Nights*! She shut her eyes briefly as she prayed for composure. But this was real life, not a play or film that she could walk away from, and she would want to walk away from this man, would need to. He was all-consuming, the antithesis of everything her instincts were telling her were right for her.

'Samantha?' She started at the name, her eyes opening wide as she looked into the gold depths of his. 'What is it?'

'I don't like that name.' She side-stepped his question intentionally. 'Samantha—I don't like it.'

'No?' He eyed her intently. 'Perhaps you had another name you were known by? Can you think what it is?'

She watched him over the rim of her glass as she took a long slow sip of wine, her eyes shuttered against the thoughts swirling in her mind, before shaking her head in the negative.

'I see.' He settled back against the low padded divan and bit into the *pastilla* in his hand, his teeth white and strong against the feather-light pastry, before fixing her with his gaze again. 'In that case, if I am not allowed to call you by the name we do know, perhaps, it would be in order to snap my fingers to get your attention?'

'Not if you expect me to respond,' she answered instantly, her hackles rising at the image his words conjured up. If he wanted a slave girl he could look elsewhere.

'Sam?' Colette entered the conversation, unaware of the subtle undercurrents. 'That's the normal abbreviation for Samantha, isn't it?'

'Not this Samantha.' Gerard's voice was a low growl. 'A woman should be called by a woman's name.'

'Well, that's a bit chauvinistic,' Kit said hotly as her eyes flashed from sister to brother. 'This is the 1990s in case you hadn't noticed. Women actually got the vote some years ago.'

'A retrograde step in my opinion,' Gerard said silkily as his eyes lingered on her hot cheeks. 'The feminist movement has a lot to answer for.'

'Why, you——' She stopped abruptly as Colette giggled at her side, and noticed the gold brown eyes surveying her so innocently were full of wicked amusement. 'You were joking,' she finished flatly, her eyes hostile even as she forced a smile.

'Was I?' His gaze never broke contact with hers as he spoke. 'Are you sure?' And now there was no amusement in the tawny depths, merely a deep searching intensity that seemed to look through into her soul. 'Do you *feel* who I am?'

'No.' She answered him in spite of herself, half mesmerised by the piercing quality of the narrowed eyes. 'I don't understand what you mean.'

'That is sad.' The room was very quiet now; even Colette seemed to realise her brother was saying more than the words held. 'To hurt someone is bad enough, but to take away their basic judgement of others borders on wickedness. The Arabs have a saying that to know oneself one must first learn to *feel* who others are. That way you accept both the good and bad, understand the imperfections so that there are no damaging surprises later to mar a relationship. It also enables one to pick out the one perfect jewel and discard the rest.'

'It's not possible to do that,' she whispered slowly.

'On the contrary.' There was no cynicism in his face now, neither could it have been called hard. 'The aura that is an essential part of each one of us cannot be denied, but too many people, especially in the Western world, look on the outward appearance, trust the dubious sincerity of mere words. The Arabs recognise that the inner soul is far more discerning. But it takes time to learn, to feel, and it is not easy; one can be hurt in the process.'

'You're talking about instinct, sixth sense, call it what you will,' she said tightly. 'That's all. There's nothing mystical about that.'

'No, I am not.' He leaned forward slightly, his body big and dark against the light cloth of the divan. 'I am talking about feeling and being, learning from every little incident that touches our heart and drawing wisdom even from the disasters. I am talking about gaining strength inside, discarding bitterness and self-pity, looking at everything through an inner light that exposes the darkness and allows us to discern things as they are so we have the choice of either accepting or letting go. To gain the gift of *feeling* who others are should humble, not exalt, and in that process one finds oneself.'

'And if you don't like what you find?' she asked practically. 'I should think finding oneself is a dodgy business.'

He stared at her for a split-second before breaking into loud unrestrained laughter, his head thrown back and his mouth wide. It was infectious. She wasn't really sure what she was smiling at but she found herself smiling just the same. 'For such a bewildered little kitten you have very sharp claws,' he said after a few moments, when he could restrain his mirth. 'That will teach me to wax philosophical when I should be eating.'

As course after course came and went she found herself pondering his words. They had touched something very deep inside her and instinctively she had hidden behind humour because the alternative was too painful. Why? She searched her memory for something, anything, but the dark oasis was complete, allowing her mind rest and tranquillity from what had harmed it even as it kept its dark secret.

As Amina placed the last dish of sweetmeats on the table to join the bowls of cherries, peaches, grapes, oranges, bananas and dates already in place, Kit knew she couldn't eat another thing. 'That was wonderful, thank you.' She smiled up at Amina and Halima as she spoke, encompassing the food with a wave of her hand. 'It was all delicious.'

Gerard spoke swiftly in Arabic to the two women, who smiled back at her, bobbing their heads in delight at her appreciation before they left for the kitchen again.

'It is a little late to telephone England now,' Gerard said quietly as Amina washed their hands with the rose-scented water some minutes later before they rose from the divans. 'You agree?'

'I'll phone tomorrow.' She was very conscious of his great height as they walked through into the internal courtyard, the sensation both physically and mentally satisfying, although the little tremors that shivered down her limbs as he took her arm were anything but.

'In that case I would be most honoured to show you the gardens.' His voice was husky and deep, the slight accent giving a sensual lift to the words that set her pulses racing even as she chastised herself for her vulnerability where this man was concerned.

'I thought you said it was late,' she said carefully as Colette called goodnight from somewhere in the house, her voice light and carefree. Had she ever been like that? Kit asked herself painfully. Somehow she didn't think she had.

'Do not argue.' His voice was mild but firm. 'You have been asleep for most of the day and would not be able to sleep again so soon. A brisk walk in the cool of the night is just what you need.'

'How do you know what I need?' she answered obstinately as the old antagonism flared. He was so sure of himself, so terrifyingly sure. What did he expect of her? A brief little affair before she left, a quick titillation of his male ego? Some men had to know that they could have any woman they liked—perhaps he was like that? He couldn't be short of female companionship, that much was for sure looking the way he did. And she was no *femme fatale*. What could he possibly see in her beyond the thrill of the chase and ultimate conquest?

'Through here.' He led her through a delicate stucco arch constructed in a wall softly coloured with mosaic tiles of different hues, and she found herself walking down a long corridor at the perimeter of the extensive kitchens at the back of the house. Amina and Halima's voice could be heard within along with that of a man, probably Assad. Abou was rarely about and when he was seemed morose and withdrawn, quite different from his smiling brother who was clearly Gerard's close friend.

Gerard opened an iron gate set in a wall of criss-cross stone, and as they passed through into the gardens she was aware of the soft balmy blanket of sky above and the sweet perfume of warm vegetation below, of the tall, exotically clothed figure at her side, his robes flowing around him as he walked, and of her own stark vulnerability that suddenly gripped her throat in a stranglehold. What was she doing? What *was* she doing? It was as though a force stronger than herself was drawing her on. The gardens were lit by strategically placed lamps and for a few minutes she forgot her fears and she drank in the beauty all around her. A delicate stream with tiny waterfalls, bordered on either side by grass and flowers, meandered through lawns shaded by weeping willows, oaks and many other trees, exotic bougainvillaeas and hibiscus vying with the heady perfume of roses, honeysuckle and jasmine and the odd bower enclosed and hidden by thick, brilliant green ivy trained over latticed wood. There must have been two acres of land in all, but the gardens were set out in such a way that it seemed far, far more.

'My mother planted most of the trees herself.' They stopped under a spreading cedar tree, its vast trunk enclosed by a circular seat of wood, which Gerard indicated with a wave of his hand. 'Most Moroccan gardens are ornamental but she preferred a more relaxed environment.'

'It's absolutely lovely.' Kit sat gingerly on the very edge of the seat, her body as tense as a rod as he sat down beside her.

'Have you remembered anything at all?' They had sat in a silence that was anything but comfortable for several minutes before Gerard spoke again, and she had never been more aware of another human being in her life. The subtle but intoxicating fragrance that emanated from the dark tanned skin, the big muscled body and narrowed glittering eyes... He was like a creature of the night, dangerous, powerful and utterly at home in his natural habitat.

'Not really,' she answered jerkily.

'Have you tried——?'

'Of course I've tried,' she interrupted sharply, as she tried to banish the intimate atmosphere of sexual awareness with out and out hostility. 'I don't like being like this, for goodness' sake.'

'I was going to say have you tried loosening up a little?' The deep voice was cool and unemotional, but as she glanced up into the impassive face she caught a little glimmer of reaction to her glance in the thickly lashed eyes moments before a curtain came down to hide their expression. He wanted her. The knowledge was a little jolt in her chest. Whatever the motive, that had been hot primitive desire in those tawny eyes.

'That's not exactly easy to do.' She drew her feet up on to the bench, clasping her knees close to her chest as she let her hair hang forward in a curtain over her flushed cheeks. 'I'm frightened.' Why she admitted that to him she didn't know; part of her wanted to remain cool and aloof but another part of her needed his hard masculine strength, his protection. Stupid, stupid, stupid, she told herself painfully. It was something far more basic than protection that was on his mind. She had to be alert, on her guard, every minute.

'Of course you are, I understand that,' he said softly. 'As I said, for a such a bewildered little kitten, you are being very brave.'

'No, you said I had sharp claws.' She tried for lightness but it didn't quite come off as her voice cracked slightly.

'It's the same thing.'

She knew he was going to kiss her and she also knew it was crazy, foolhardy, but she wanted him to. He terrified her, intimidated and threatened her in a way she didn't understand, but there was something stronger than all that turning her face up to meet his as his hand cupped her chin in a gentle hold. It was a deep, long, sensual kiss, and even as she felt her body respond the thought came that she wasn't ready for this. She struggled slightly as his arm enclosed her back, moving her intimately against him, but his body was like iron, immovable. He was very experienced. Even as the thought took hold she found herself relaxing in his embrace as his lips caressed her cheeks and ears, moving over her eyes with feather-like kisses that began a trembling deep inside she couldn't hide. And then he took her mouth again and she found her lips parting to allow him entry as her hands held on to the bulk of his hard muscled shoulders.

'You taste like honey.' The whisper brushed her skin with a million little sensations that were pure magic. 'So sweet, so very sweet.' She felt his warm hand on the skin under her top but was powerless to stop him, her breasts tightening and filling at his touch until she felt as though she would explode. He had told her during dinner that she was twenty-five years old, engaged to be married, and yet if she hadn't known better she would have sworn this was the first time she had been touched like this. As she felt the cool night air on her aching breasts she realised he had opened her top, his eyes feasting where his hands had wandered, and immediately a sense of shame and shock coupled with a deep ignominy at her lack of inches had her covering her body with her hands.

'Don't do that; you are beautiful.' Even as his voice spoke her mind repudiated the husky words. Beautiful? With her slender boyish body and small breasts? She shut her eyes against the ridicule and pity she felt she would see on his face. 'Kitten? Open your eyes.'

'No.' She tried to move away, to escape from the big body trapping hers, but he merely seized the opportunity to fit her more closely against him.

'What is it?' Her hands were trapped between her own body and the wall of his chest now, and she could feel coarse curling body hair where his tunic had fallen open baring his muscled torso. The sensation caused a raw panic as the reality of his masculinity pressed in on her, the knowledge of what he could do to her if he tried suddenly alarmingly real. 'What is wrong?'

'Please let me go.' She opened big tortured grey eyes to stare into the narrowed gold of his. 'Please.'

'There is no need to be ashamed of your body.' His voice was soft but with a steel thread of persistence that she recognised as inflexible. 'You are a very lovely young woman; this cannot all be so new to you.'

'Gerard...' She shook her head desperately like a tiny wild animal caught in a steel-jawed trap. 'Please.'

'Who has hurt you like this?' He relaxed his hold sufficiently for her to free her hands and button the blouse with shaking fingers, and then moved her chin to face him again, his touch gentle. 'I want you, kitten, you know that,' he said slowly, his voice thick and husky, 'but I can wait.'

'I'm——' Her voice cracked and she took a deep breath to try again, the feel of his arms round her making her shiver. 'I'm engaged to be married, *you said*.'

'But you are not married yet.' The light brown eyes narrowed and became hard. 'And whoever this David is, he has not made you happy or you would not be here now.'

'I'm here because of an accident,' she protested faintly as he stroked back the hair from her hot forehead, his eyes reflective.

'No, not the accident.' His face tightened. 'You have to face that, kitten. You are here because of something you want to forget, something that has hurt you so badly that your mind has taken refuge in the only way it knows how. If you were mine you would not have had to do this.'

'That's ridiculous.' The sheer arrogance of the statement sent a flood of welcome adrenaline into her limbs, quelling the humiliating shaking. 'How can you possibly say that?'

'Because of the way you react in my arms even as you are trying to fight me.' There was something almost menacing in the tanned features now. 'You want me although you are determined to deny us both. Is this not true?'

'I don't even know you!' she said in amazement. 'And I don't know what sort of women you are used to, but I don't fall into bed at the drop of a hat.'

'Who was talking about bed?' He moved her more closely against him, kissing the tip of her nose with warm lips. 'I am not a callow youth who has to prove himself by the act of possession. I thought we were getting to know each other a little, giving and receiving pleasure?' He stroked the side of her face with one finger, his touch tender. 'I have no intention of doing anything you do not like, kitten.'

'But——' As she began to speak he covered her lips with his own, kissing her long and hard as he enclosed her in the circle of his arms. Why did he have to be so good at this? she asked herself faintly as a river of hot smooth sensation flooded every nerve and sinew. Wonderfully, frighteningly good? How many women had he *had*, for crying out loud?

'Relax...' As his mouth moved to her throat and ears she felt her head go back to allow him greater access, her submission being met by a low growl in the base of his throat that thrilled and excited her, but he made no move to take the lovemaking any further than before and she sensed he wouldn't even as her hands fluttered in helpless protest as he touched her skin. He returned almost immediately to her mouth, kissing her for a long time, his lips and tongue teasing, provocative and sensual in turn until she began to think it was impossible to contain the emotions he was arousing. And then, quite suddenly, he stopped.

'What's wrong?' She opened dazed eyes to stare up into his face as he held her against him, his touch more restrictive than demanding now.

'I think that is enough getting to know each other for now,' he said gruffly, and as she caught the slight shake in his voice her eyes widened. He wasn't so much in control as he would have her believe, she thought, with a little thrill of excitement.

'It is?' The knowledge that she could arouse a man such as this was intoxicating.

'It is.' He eyed her drily. 'Unless you are prepared for me to lay you out on the grass and take you?' Her eyes dropped from his and he smiled sardonically. 'Exactly. So if we are presuming that discretion is the better part of valour, here endeth the first lesson.' As he leant across and adjusted her clothing with steady impersonal fingers before rising and drawing her up beside him, the sudden realisation that she had been playing with fire came hot and strong. The strength was all his, the sheer physical power totally in his court. If he had lost control... She glanced up into his face inches above her, noting the massive powerful shoulders and broad chest with a little shiver deep inside. She must have been crazy, mad—what was the matter with her, courting disaster like this? Was there some sort of drug in the air? And why was he bothering with her in the first place?

Because she was available? The answer came from deep within and hurt more than she could say. He was obviously a sensual, virile man well skilled in the arts of love. He must have women clamouring for his attention, beautiful sexy women who would know exactly how to please a man of the world like him. But he was here on his estate at the moment and she was the only woman around. He knew she would be leaving soon, that there would of necessity be no strings attached to a light affair with her even if she wasn't what he would normally choose. 'I prefer my women with a little more meat on their bones and definitely more submissive.' The words he had thrown at her a few days before came back with stark clarity. Oh, how could she have been such a fool?

She didn't speak again on the way back to the house, and fortunately he seemed lost in a world of his own, holding her hand loosely as they passed through the arch into the warm interior and only coming to himself as they reached the bottom of the long winding staircase. 'Kitten——'

She interrupted him harshly, the thoughts that had tormented her for the last few minutes making her painfully aware of her physical shortcomings. 'Don't call me that.'

'What?' The slight smile died on his lips as the narrowed gold eyes registered the naked hostility apparent in both her body and face.

'Kitten. I'm not your kitten or anyone else's,' she said tightly. 'Just because——' She stopped abruptly.

'Because?' Afterwards she realised she should have been warned by that silky smoothness in his voice but at the time it just hadn't registered on her angry mind.

'Because we exchanged a few kisses, you needn't think I'm ready to fall into your bed,' she said flatly.

'Fall into my bed?' He stood back a pace, crossing his arms as he did so and looking fleetingly like an imperious sultan faced with a rebellious slave, as the long Arab robes flowed round the powerful body and his tawny brown hair gleamed in the light from the oil lamp above his head. 'Is it not customary to wait to be asked?'

'I didn't mean——' She stopped abruptly. 'I wasn't *offering*,' she finished harshly.

'Good.' He eyed her with dispassionate coldness. 'Because you would have been turned down. I don't bed on the first date either.'

He had left her before she could retaliate, left her standing at the bottom of the ornately carved staircase as he disappeared into the labyrinth of a house without a backward glance.

CHAPTER FIVE

KIT slept very badly. Whether it was due to the fact that she had slept most of the day away or the molten anger that seethed in her chest like lava, or, and she had to admit to herself the last point was the most likely, the raging, over-powering sensations that Gerard's body had called forth from hers, she wasn't sure. Whatever, dawn was already touching the night sky with mauve-tipped fingers when at last she slept only to be awakened two hours later by a bright-faced Amina and a strong cup of coffee. '*Sbah el khir*?' At her dazed gaze the small Moroccan woman giggled with her hand over her mouth in apology. 'Is the good morning, yes? Go down now, *now*?'

'You want me to go downstairs?' Kit demonstrated the import of her words with a wave of her hands to which Amina responded with a vigorous nod. '*Waha*, yes, yes. Down. You eat.'

Breakfast, at this time of the morning? She glanced at her watch wearily. It was only six o'clock. Did they always eat so early here?

When she walked into the dining-room ten minutes later after a hasty shower, her hair damp, it was to find Gerard sitting behind a newspaper at the end of the massive room with a small breakfast-table loaded with bowls of sliced fruit and small loaves of Arab bread and preserves in front of him. The whole scene was in such contrast to the Eastern atmosphere of the night before that she was lost for words as she joined him.

'Good morning.' The newspaper lowered at her approach and she saw the mode of dress had changed to a casual shirt and cotton trousers replacing the flowing robes of the day before, but in no way diminishing the raw sex appeal that oozed from the big frame as his eyes ran casually over her slender form, encased in her own clothes that Amina had washed and ironed and replaced in the wardrobe in her room. 'You'll need to change before we leave.'

'Leave?' Just for a minute she thought he was telling her she was being dispatched back to Casablanca that day, and the harsh jolt her heart gave unnerved her more than his words.

'It would seem in view of the developments of yesterday that your time in Marrakesh is limited,' he said impassively as Amina arrived with a pot of steaming coffee and a large jug of freshly squeezed orange juice. 'No doubt David will want you to join him as soon as possible.' The hard gold gaze was quite unreadable. 'In view of this I thought it would be advisable to show you a little of my country before you leave to return to your old life. This is acceptable to you? Of course, Colette would have been the perfect choice but she is otherwise engaged,' he continued smoothly, 'but no matter.'

'Oh, right . . .' It was too early and she had had too little sleep to enter into a battle of words and besides, she caught the thought abruptly but it had already taken form, she wanted a day with him.

He waited a moment for further comment and when none was forthcoming leant slightly forward, his male warmth seeming to encompass her air space although he was several inches from touching her. 'It would probably be better if you wore a long skirt and a blouse that covers all of your arms,' he said quietly. 'The Moslem religion expects this of its women, and although you are not bound by such things it would be considered an act of politeness, a respect of local customs.'

'Yes, of course.' She nodded stiffly. 'Would it be in order for me to phone England when I've eaten?'

'It is a little early, do you not think?' he said smoothly. 'We shall return in time for dinner tonight so perhaps it would be more . . . considerate to make the call then?'

She looked straight at him and held the cool shuttered gaze for a long moment before nodding again. 'All right.' Why didn't he want her to phone David? she asked herself silently as she helped herself to a bowl of freshly sliced watermelon. What possible reason could he have? She began to eat mechanically, her thoughts far away. Did he think the longer she was kept from outside influences the more chance he would have of seducing her? And just how long, exactly, did he intend her to stay here anyway? It had been meant as a refuge until her identity could be established, but surely that didn't apply any more?

'It has been very kind of you to let me stay here,' she began carefully as her thoughts prompted her to speak, 'but now we know who I am I don't want to impose on your hospitality any longer——'

'Rubbish.' The word was sharp and immediate and she blinked at him as he glared at her across the table. 'You have been *told* who you are but as far as I am concerned the situation has not altered. You are still unable to remember even the most elementary facts about your past life. For all we know this David could have ill-treated you, beaten you even; perhaps it is him you were running from.'

'I hardly think so.' She stared at him, surprised by the force of emotion in the dark face.

'You hardly think so.' He repeated her words with a bitingly cool mockery that brought immediate colour into her pale cheeks. 'And why do you hardly think so?'

'Because I don't think I'd put up with treatment like that from anyone,' she said hotly, her eyes flashing, 'least of all someone I'm engaged to.'

'Perhaps not.' He seemed to take a pull of air and almost force himself to speak moderately. 'But until you can speak from what you know and not from supposition, I think it advisable you remain here. The doctors assure me it is usually a matter of days in these cases when no physical injury is involved. It only needs one spark and you will be as before. Besides——' his face was expressionless now although the beautiful eyes were piercing on her face '—you hardly seem to be pining for this David.'

'I can't remember him, can I?' she answered sharply.

'Exactly.'

By the time they left the house nearly an hour later the dry sunny air was redolent with the scents of rosemary and jasmine and full of bird song from the fruit trees lining the drive, and as the powerful Ferrari passed through the gates on to the dusty road outside, the dominating minaret of the Koutoubia Mosque, 77 metres high, was clearly visible in the crystal-clear, startlingly blue sky.

As they took the main road to Taroudant out of Marrakesh, Kit was acutely aware of the big male body next to hers in the close confines of the car and quite unable to relax, alive to every slight movement of the capable brown hands on the steering-wheel, every small movement of his head as he checked traffic and negotiated manoeuvres in the already considerable traffic.

They drove in silence for some time until after about half an hour had ticked by in uneasy quiet and the car had begun to climb in gentle spirals alongside the rushing torrent of icy water that made up the Ourika river, Gerard suddenly spoke. 'You are making me nervous.'

'What?' Her head spun to the handsome profile but he concentrated on the road ahead, his mouth slightly twisted at the note of surprise in her voice.

'I said you are making me nervous with this fidgety edginess and anxious face.' Now the clear gold-brown eyes did stroke her face fleetingly for one swift moment before returning to the windscreen. 'What is it you expect of me that you are so apprehensive, kitten?'

'I don't expect anything,' she answered weakly, the clean sensual smell of his aftershave registering on her taut nerves like fire.

'This is good.' He spared her another swift glance, his eyes narrowed and alive with mocking amusement. 'I was beginning to worry that I could not live up to your expectations as a—how you say—Casanova?'

'Oh, you...' Her voice trailed away as an adequate description failed her.

'I know, I am the savage, eh?' he asked with comfortable derision, his soft warm chuckle turning her limbs to melted jelly.

'I don't think you're a savage,' she answered carefully, trying to concentrate without success on the view out of the car window, its grandeur almost completely wasted on her as all her senses tuned in to his magnetic pull.

'No?' He was silent for a moment, his mouth serious when he spoke again. 'And what exactly *do* you think I am, my little English kitten, eh?'

'I'm not sure.' She glanced fleetingly at the hard profile and then turned her gaze back to safer subjects again. 'I think you're kind; you've been kind to me.'

'Kind?' If she had called him the devil incarnate he couldn't have been more furious, she reflected miserably, as the car swerved violently for a second before resuming its steady course.

'Old women are kind,' he said scathingly, running a hand through the tawny mane of his hair with a gesture that spoke of his outrage far more adequately than any words could have done.

'I didn't mean——' She stopped abruptly.

'Yes?' he asked intimidatingly.

'I didn't mean you weren't other things as well.' The air was suddenly prickly, charged with an electricity that sent small shivers flying down her spine.

'Such as?' he asked silkily, his voice soft.

'Well...' Hell's bells, this was *awful*, she thought helplessly as her cheeks became still hotter. What on earth did he expect her to say anyway? That she thought he was the most fantastic man she had ever seen? That one look from those amazing eyes and she was a trembling mess? She caught herself abruptly, surprised and alarmed at the way her mind was moving. 'I'm not going to tell you,' she said with sudden firmness. 'You're big-headed enough as it is.'

'I'm...?' The blank silence caused her breath to stop in her throat before he chuckled again a moment later. 'OK, you win that round, kitten.' She wasn't fooled by the apparent capitulation and sure enough a second later he spoke again, his voice deep and soft. 'But I take it I wouldn't have been too displeased by your summing-up?'

'You can take what you want,' she said tartly, regretting the import of her reply the second it left her lips.

'There's no answer to that.' She could hear dark amusement throbbing in the deep voice and would have loved to fire back with an appropriately scathing rejoinder, but her mind just refused to co-operate. 'Look, if I promise to behave would you at least try and enjoy yourself?' he asked a moment later, glancing at her hands clenched in tight fists on her lap. 'This is a wonderful spot and I would like you to appreciate it.'

'Yes, well...' She heard her voice with a definite feeling of self-disgust. What *did* she sound like! Moronic! 'Yes, all right,' she said more firmly. 'A truce?'

'A truce,' he agreed gravely, the slight quiver in the richly accented voice causing her to look at him suspiciously, but the tanned handsome face was quite expressionless and devoid of all humour.

As the car sped on, eating up the miles with careless disregard, she was entranced to see hanging on the almost vertical sides of the valley, tiny villages that were difficult to spot from any distance, being made of the same rich red earth as the valley itself, but were picturesque in the extreme.

'They look wildly romantic,' Gerard said quietly at her side, reading her mind accurately, 'but I have it on good authority they are murder to live in.'

'Are they?' She tried to picture the peaceful isolated life the villagers must lead. 'I wouldn't care.'

'With the right company, neither would I,' he said softly, a subtle inflexion in his voice bringing the colour surging into her face.

Why did he have to say things like that, she asked herself crossly, and, more to the point, why did she always have to respond on cue? She *knew* this was all a game, a momentary diversion out of his normal routine of business; why couldn't she at least pretend coolness? She was still seething quietly some time later, when the car passed through a little hamlet and came to a halt as the road petered to a finish in deference to the breathtaking majesty of the gorge.

'We walk from this point,' Gerard said comfortably as she looked at him expectantly. 'Amina has packed a picnic in the back of the car and we will eat shortly.'

'But...' She glanced round at the bottomless ravine and soaring peaks of the mountains above, suddenly feeling very tiny and very vulnerable. They could have been the only people in the world.

'No buts, my timid little kitten,' he said mockingly, laughing softly as she flashed him a furious glance of such venom that it rendered his description null and void. 'Here, you take the rug and I will bring the hamper, yes?'

They found a spot she was sure he had had specially made for a seduction scene, the grass a thick flowery carpet of hundreds of wild flowers with an ancient cypress tree providing welcome shade from the heat of the sun, although the soft warm breeze kept the temperature comfortable. As he spread the rug out under the green branches she found that her stomach was clenched into a giant knot, her nerves as tight as piano wire. 'Come and sit down,' he said mildly, his eyes narrowed against the sun as he glanced up at her standing rigid and still to one side of the blanket. 'What would you like to eat?'

'I——' She gestured with her hand abruptly as she sank down on to the warm rug. 'Anything, anything,' she said jerkily.

'Come here.' His voice was suddenly very low and very tender as he stared into her troubled face, and as she made no move to approach him he rolled over to her, sitting up to face her as he reached her side. 'I am not going to hurt you, kitten,' he said patiently as he cupped her face in his large brown hands. 'When are you going to believe that? We are going to eat, maybe talk a little, let the sun warm us and just enjoy the moment. Now——' he smiled slowly '—you can be mother.' He indicated the hamper with a lazy wave of his hand. 'Wait on me, wench.'

They feasted on the hundred and one little delicacies Amina had packed so carefully: tiny mouthwatering pasties filled with ground meat, chopped hard-boiled eggs, cheese and vegetables, small spiced lamb sausages, lemon chicken dipped in melted brown sugar, succulent prawns and tender lobster, fresh green salad, nutty Arab rolls and freshly baked croissants, besides every imaginable fruit Kit could think of and all washed down with a rich fruity red wine that tasted of honey and summer days.

'I'm going to burst.' Kit ran a lazy hand over the swell of her stomach. 'I couldn't eat another thing.' The good food and three large glassfuls of wine she had consumed had made her limbs like lead, and as Gerard moved close, turning her into his body so that her head was lying on his broad chest and her limbs were stretched along the length of his, she found she was powerless to resist.

'Go to sleep,' he said softly, kissing the top of her head as he settled her more comfortably against him, the feel of his hard muscled body producing a sensual warmth that was intoxicatingly good. 'You are tipsy.'

'Tipsy?' She tried for indignation but the emotion just wasn't there. What she wanted more than anything else was to have him make love to her. The thought should have shocked, but it merely tantalised and she realised he was right. She *was* tipsy. She giggled softly against the hard bulk of his chest. 'Did you do this on purpose?'

'Do what?' He moved her slightly to stare down into her flushed face. 'If you remember, my greedy little kitten, you poured the last two glasses of wine yourself.'

'So I did.' She giggled again. 'But you didn't stop me.'

'I'm no saint.' As he touched her mouth with his own, his big body turning to crouch over her, she gave herself up to the kiss with uninhibited pleasure, but after a long moment of his mouth devouring hers he moved back to his original position with a deep groan. 'Go to sleep, kitten.'

'Why?' She knew she was behaving badly but she didn't care. She was so tired of being frightened and lonely and defensive. She wanted... She wanted *him*.

'Because when I have you you will be fully *compos mentis*, my English siren, and you will want me with your mind as well as your body,' he said grimly.

'I do now,' she protested weakly, her head spinning.

'You think you do.' He raised himself on one elbow, and as her head rested on the thick grass she looked up into the tanned face above her but his features were a hazy golden shadow in the brilliance of the sun. 'But the wine has merely lowered the drawbridge temporarily; we cannot always rely on such a thing. This is how you should be, how you want to be, the real you, but you have to find that yourself with no outward stimulus and then, then you will be the woman you were meant to be.'

'But——' She stopped abruptly, her brow wrinkling. 'I'm going home soon, aren't I? There's David...'

'Damn David!' As she started at the savagery in his voice he caught her to him again, his voice soft. 'I am sorry, do not be afraid. But forget David for now, concentrate on me. I shall not let you go until you know yourself, kitten, however long that takes.' There was something in his voice she didn't understand, something she needed to comprehend. She stared up at him with huge drowning eyes, and he shook his head slowly as his mouth moved to take hers again. 'Dammit, but you are making this hard, so rich and ripe and honey-soft...' He was breathing hard now, his body rigid with control as he plundered her mouth with his, his tongue plunging and filling and tasting until she thought she would go mad with the sensations he was producing, his hands sliding over her body in an agony of hot desire as he held her to him, his arousal blatant and fierce against the softness of her thighs.

'Hell, woman!' As he wrenched his mouth from hers and rolled roughly from her she lay quivering and trembling, her body feverishly alive and aching with an alien need that made her aware of every part of her anatomy.

'Gerard——'

'No, don't, don't say a word,' he said harshly as he stood up in one violent movement and walked to stand some yards away, his hands palm down on a large boulder as he bent to take deep steady breaths, his back to her. 'You see? I have little control where you are concerned.'

They remained locked in a frozen tableau for long minutes until he straightened, walking back to the picnic hamper and taking a long hard pull of the iced water he had drunk after allowing himself just one glass of wine. 'It is getting late.' He glanced at his watch and then met her troubled stare with a purposefully blank face. 'I want to return in time for the entertainment in

Djemaa-el-Fna square, so perhaps we should leave now.'

'Gerard?' Her voice was a tiny whisper as the events of the last few minutes began to nullify the influence of the wine. 'What have I done wrong?'

'Nothing.' His voice was rueful with a dark amusement containing biting self-mockery. 'It is just a little disconcerting when one meets one's Waterloo, kitten.'

'I don't understand,' she said bewilderedly.

'That is probably just as well.' He eyed her grimly. 'But just trust me when I say it's time to leave, that's all.'

She must have slept on the way back, the lack of sleep the night before coupled with the relaxing effect of the wine producing a deep dreamless stupor from which she roused herself with difficulty as they drew into a side road approaching Djemaa-el-Fna square, the dusky half-light illuminated by flickering gas-lights which mellowed the ancient castellated ramparts around the old town.

'All right?' Gerard's voice was soft as he glanced at her and she sat up sharply in the seat as he stopped the car. As she met his veiled eyes the events of the afternoon came rushing back with humiliating clearness. She had thrown herself at him! Quite literally thrown herself at him. She wanted to close her eyes to blot out his face, but forced herself to answer in a normal voice that betrayed none of her inner agitation.

'Fine, thank you.' She smiled brightly. 'And you?'

'I also am fine,' he said quietly, his face deadpan. He indicated the street with a wave of his hand. 'Shall we?'

As they approached the square it was the noise and smells that registered first, the whole gigantic sideshow of snake-charmers, sword-swallowers, fire-eaters, musicians with painted fiddles and rattle snare drums, dancers, beggars, scribes sitting under umbrellas with the tools of their trade scattered around them, spellbinders, mystics, all too much to take in at first sight. Charcoal grills on which tiny fish sizzled were scattered among vendors peddling daggers, hashish pipes, Koranic texts and a hundred and one other items, not least violently coloured portraits of the royal family.

She was supremely grateful for Gerard's solid bulk at the side of her and his arm round her waist, his stamp of ownership welcome in the ever-flowing wave of humanity all around them. She glanced up at him under her eyelashes as they wandered through the crowds, wondering what he was thinking behind the impassive, slightly cynical face he presented to the world. Did the feel of her body next to his affect him as fiercely as it did her? He felt her glance and looked down, smiling lazily before letting his gaze rove over the crowd again over which he towered by a good few inches. She doubted it. She doubted it very much indeed.

By the time they had strolled through the *souks*, the entrance to which was in one corner of the square, watching the craftsmen at work gilding on leather and inlaying with enamel the sheaths of ornate silver daggers while others hammered out copper or smoothed cedar-wood, evening was being ushered in by the long wailing song of the *muezzins* calling the faithful to prayer. Many were answering the call, drifting away from the activity in the square for meditation in the mosques, and as Gerard led her back in the direction of the car the riot of colour, noise and bustle was beginning to die.

'I've had a wonderful day.' As he opened her door and she slid into the warm interior of the car, she smiled up at Gerard carefully.

'Good.' He rested both hands on the top of the vehicle as he bent to stare in at her, his eyes slanted. 'And you will inform your David of this when you call?'

'What?' As she met his gaze she saw the tawny eyes were very clear and very hard.

'I asked if you will tell your...fiancé how much you enjoyed this day.' He shut her door abruptly and moved round to join her in the car.

'Of course I will.' The few seconds had given her time to recover from the direct attack.

'And do you not think he will consider it strange that you are not missing him, that you have spent the day quite happily in another man's company?' He reached out and smoothed a strand of silky chestnut red hair from her cheek, his touch possessive. She forced herself not to flinch, to show no reaction at all as his skin touched hers.

'I don't see why he should.' She stared back at him, her face both defensive and vulnerable.

'No?' He shook his head slowly as he bent to brush her lips with his own before turning into his seat and starting the engine with a flick of his hand. 'Then you are either as naïve and untouched as I am beginning to think, or capable of a callousness that puts me to shame. If I had been foolish enough to let you leave my side I would have killed the first man who looked at you with desire in his heart.' His voice was so cool, so deliberate, that for a moment the impact of the statement didn't register on her mind, and when it did the tingling shiver that flickered down her spine left a trail of sensual warmth that sent the blood surging into her cheeks.

'That's ridiculous.' She fastened her seatbelt with shaking fingers and prayed for aplomb.

'No.' His voice was a low growl. 'That is——' He stopped abruptly and time ticked by for an endless second in breathless savagery. 'That is something quite different.' And then the powerful car sprang into life and as Gerard eased it into the crowded street she found she was still holding her breath in tense expectation.

They reached Del Mahari within minutes, and as Gerard led her into his beautiful book-lined study to make the call to England she prayed he would leave. He didn't. As he seated himself behind the massive cedar-wood desk and spoke to the operator, organising the call, she felt her knees grow weak and sank down into the seat he had indicated with a fearful heart. How would she feel when she heard this David's voice? A voice she must know very well?

'Here.' As Gerard passed the phone to her she took it with a trembling hand. 'It is ringing.'

'Hello? Emma speaking.' The bright voice seemed vaguely familiar but that was all.

'Emma?' She took a deep breath as Gerard picked up some papers from his desk and appeared to be engrossed in their contents. 'It's me. Samantha,' she added uncomfortably.

'Samantha!' The bright voice took on a note of incredulity. 'Since when did you call yourself that? Oh, sorry...' There was a clear moment of embarrassment. 'I forgot. Darling, how *are* you? We've all been worried to death here. Can you remember anything yet?'

'Not really.' Kit took a deep breath. 'Look, I know this might seem a strange question but what *do* I call myself, Emma?'

'Kit.' The disembodied voice at the other end of the phone answered immediately. 'You call yourself Kit. You hate Samantha.' There was a moment of awkward silence and then Emma's voice spoke again, her tone tentative. 'Look, Kit, there are a few things I ought to tell you; can you——?' The next second there was a noise almost as though the phone had been dropped and then a man's deep tones took over.

'Kit? It's David. I've practically lived here for the last twenty-four hours waiting for your call.'

'Have you?' The voice was almost a whine with a definite note of complaint in its depths, and it did nothing for her, nothing at all. She glanced across at Gerard, who was quite still behind the desk, his whole attention seemingly concentrated on the papers in front of him. She searched for something, anything, to say. 'How are you, David?'

'How am I?' Now the grievance became more clear. 'How the hell do you think I am, Kit? You disappear on holiday without letting any of us know where you're going and you ask me how I am?' There was the sound of a woman's voice in the background and when David spoke again his tone was more moderate, a note of concern forced into the peevishness. 'Anyway, enough of that. You still can't remember anything, then?'

'Not really.'

'Tough luck, old girl. What happened exactly?' As she explained the circumstances of the accident she waited for the inevitable question, and when it came she took a deep breath before answering.

'Yes, David, I'm still at the home of Gerard Dumont. He has been very kind.' The papers on the desk rustled abruptly but were immediately stilled.

'Oh, yeah?' There followed a pregnant pause. 'And how old is this Good Samaritan, anyway?'

'I really can't go into that now,' she said carefully. 'Perhaps next time I call.'

'Next time?' The snivelling content of his voice rang a bell, but not long enough for her to hold on to the image. 'Emma and I thought you'd be coming back now—there's no need to stay, is there? We've made it clear to the authorities we'll pay for your ticket home if your bag isn't found——'

'There's no need for that, David. Fortunately I'd left my passport and ticket and some other papers in the hotel safe. There couldn't have been much in my bag when it was taken. The police told Mr Dumont everything is in order.'

'Right. When are you coming home then?' he asked immediately.

'Soon.' She took a deep breath. 'I can't be more specific.'

'I miss you, Kit.' He had obviously decided to try another tack. 'I miss you badly, sweetheart. Are you missing me?' There was the sound of Emma's voice in the background and then he spoke again. 'Oh, sorry, silly question in the circumstances. Still, I am your fiancé, Kit. You do remember that much?'

'I suppose so.' Her head was beginning to thud; this was a hundred times worse than she had imagined.

'Then say you love me.' She met the request with a blank silence. 'Please, Kit, even if you can't remember, just say it for me.'

'I can't, David.' The refusal was wrenched out of her. 'But perhaps when I see you?'

'All right.' The word was sulky, and somehow the tone brought that flash of disturbing imagery again, prompting her next words.

'Why wasn't I wearing a ring, David?' There was absolute silence for a long moment at the other end of the phone and she thought for a second they had been disconnected. 'David? Are you there? Did I have a ring?'

'Yes.' His voice was smooth now, smooth and pleasant with the sort of artificial patience one used with a young child who was being unintentionally obtuse. 'But it's at the jeweller's, sweetheart; the stone had become a little loose.'

'Had it?' She wrinkled her forehead slowly as a picture flashed into her mind. It was a diamond ring, a beautiful diamond ring and she was handing it to someone... But the emotion that came with the image was one of disgust and rage, fury even. 'Was it a diamond solitaire?'

'That's it.' His voice was uneasy now and she wondered why.

'Well, this must be costing your Mr Dumont a fortune, Kit, I'd better let you go now.' There was a brief pause. 'I love you, sweetheart.'

'Yes, goodbye, David.' She couldn't, she just *couldn't* say she loved him back. 'I'll ring you with the flight arrangements as soon as I know them.'

She replaced the receiver slowly without looking at the big silent figure sitting at the desk, and turned to walk out of the room, her head whirling. She hadn't felt a thing beyond mild confusion when talking to that person and yet, if what he said was true and there was no reason why he should lie, she had promised to spend the rest of her life with him some time in the past.

She couldn't go on living like this, she just couldn't. There must be something the doctors could do?

'Well?' Gerard's tight cold voice stopped her in her tracks. 'What do they call you, anyway?'

'Kit.' She turned to face him, her eyes stormy at his abrasive tone. 'They call me Kit. Apparently I like it.'

He made a sound of acknowledgement in his throat as he stood up and walked towards her, his eyes narrowed on her pale face. 'It would seem my "kitten" is not too far removed from what you like after all?' She said nothing, sensing a thick, angry force vibrating from the taut body that was being held in check by an iron will. 'But of course it is not David who is calling you that, is it?' he said flatly as she continued to face him. 'That would obviously make a difference.'

'I suppose so.' She shrugged carefully, uncertain of how to react.

'You suppose so.' He nodded slowly. 'And the oh, so concerned, ever-attentive David? Has he explained why he was not on the first plane out here when he heard about your accident?'

'What?' She stared at him in confusion.

'Do not tell me the thought had not occurred to you?' he asked coolly.

'No, it hadn't.' The ring of honesty in her voice was so obviously genuine he had to believe her.

'You mean to tell me that this kind of lukewarm emotion that the man is displaying is satisfactory to you?' he asked, incredulously. 'I do not believe it.'

'I don't know about being satisfactory,' she said slowly as her brow wrinkled as she searched for words to explain what she was feeling. 'I think it's just that I've always been used to being on my own, sorting out my own problems.' She stared at him as the concept became a firm conviction. 'I don't expect anyone to take care of me,' she finished quietly, 'I don't think they ever have.'

'*Mon dieu* . . .' He took her wrists in a biting grip, his face suddenly dark with a fierce emotion he couldn't hide. 'You should expect it! Hell . . .' He shook her slightly, his eyes fiery. 'And you expect me to let you leave to go back to that? There is something wrong here, something very wrong.'

'I have David.' Why she said it she didn't know because it was the very worst thing possible.

'David?' The dark face was suddenly icy, thick brows lifting in insultingly cool contradiction. 'Oh, but of course, the English David.' In the split-second before his mouth came down hard on hers she felt pure fear, and then a rush of harsh pleasure drove every other emotion out of her mind. Kit was crushed against the hardness of his body as his mouth became more demanding, a low growling sound in his throat as he ravaged hers before returning to her open lips, his strong hands running over her body and leaving fire wherever they touched.

'And your David?' he asked harshly as he raised his head briefly, his eyes glittering. 'Do you think he can make you feel like this, respond to him like this?'

'I don't know,' she moaned softly as the hard driving pressure of his mouth sent her into a whirlwind of sensual pleasure.

'Well, I do.' He held her from him, his breathing ragged. 'You would not forget *me* so easily, kitten; you would not forget me at all.'

'I would——'

'Like hell,' he said softly, his eyes a brilliant unnerving gold and his mouth cruel. 'Like hell, kitten. I am not letting you go.'

As she wrenched herself from him and ran from the room she heard him say her name once before she reached the stairs, but continued her headlong dash until she reached the sanctuary of her room to fall breathless and shaking on to the bed.

What did he want from her? The thought mocked her as soon as it formed. She knew what he *wanted*! She flicked on the bedside lamp and padded across to the long full-length mirror on the other side of the room dazedly. But why? What was it that attracted him? She wasn't beautiful, she knew she wasn't beautiful, and the idea that he intended to enjoy a brief affair because she was available just didn't hold water the more she thought about it. She had seen how he drew every female eye today, seen it and hated it. He would have no problem in clicking his fingers and having every woman within a fifty mile radius come running!

It could only be that he thought she was playing hard to get, that he was enjoying the chase, the breaking down of her defences, she thought wearily. That had to be it. She crossed the room and flung herself on to the bed, her head pounding and her chest tight with unshed tears. And she hated him for it, she did. She ground her teeth in an agony of pain. *She did*.

She lay for long minutes in the shadowed cool room, determined not to cry, eventually rousing herself as a soft timid knock sounded at the closed door. She padded across and opened it without speaking to see Halima standing on the threshold, a loaded tray in her hands. 'You like eat here?' the Moroccan woman asked hesitantly. 'I bring, yes?'

'Thank you, Halima.' As Kit stood aside for the other woman to enter she flicked on the light switch at the side of the door to add to the dim light from the bedside lamp, and as Halima walked past her Kit couldn't stop a gasp of shock at the huge bruise marring all one side of Halima's pretty face. 'Halima?' She caught the woman's arm, causing her to turn to face her fully. 'What on earth have you done?'

'I no understand.' Halima's eyes dropped from hers to face the floor. 'You eat, yes?'

'Blow the food.' She took the tray quickly, placing it on the bed. 'Your face, Halima?' She touched her own cheek in explanation. 'What have you done?'

'I fall.' Still the other woman didn't raise her eyes. 'I go now.'

'You fell?' There was something wrong here. As the hairs on the back of Kit's neck rose in an eerie shiver she had the bizarre feeling she had been in this situation before, had the same conversation. 'How, where?'

'I no understand.' As Halima's soft brown eyes rose to look into hers Kit's heart pounded at the mute appeal in their liquid depths. Halima understood all right but there was something stopping her speaking. 'I go now.'

'Please, Halima.' Kit took her arm as she made to leave. 'How did this happen?' Halima didn't fall. The knowledge was uncanny but unmistakable and, as the thought solidified, Kit found herself beginning to tremble. She knew without a doubt Halima hadn't fallen. Someone had done this to her, hurt her, but how did Kit know that?

'I go.' This time Kit didn't stop her, but as the door closed she stood for a long time staring into space, icy little trickles of fear running up and down her spine. She had to remember, this was important. *She had to.* She drove her clenched fists against the side of her head in frustrated pain as her mind refused to give up its secret. This was the key to her amnesia here in her hand, but how did she find the door it fitted?

CHAPTER SIX

THE call for breakfast came at the sedate time of nine o'clock the next morning and Kit was amazed to find she had slept the night away. She hadn't expected to, she reflected ruefully as she luxuriated under the smooth warm flow of the shower, but the mental and physical exhaustion that had had her in its grip had acted as nature's sedative. Nevertheless, her stomach was churning unpleasantly when she walked nervously into the sunny breakfast-room only to find it empty. She reprimanded herself instantly for the thud of disappointment.

'Hi . . .' Colette joined her a moment later, the brilliant copper hair secured in a high ponytail on the top of her head and her small, slim body clothed in a loose flowing caftan. 'You were early birds yesterday.' The slanted green eyes rested briefly on Kit's warm face. 'Enjoy the day out?'

'Yes, thank you.' Kit aimed for a non-committal smile. 'Tiring, though.'

'I bet.' Colette nodded understandingly. 'Well, you're off the hook today. Gerard's already left for the new part of Marrakesh to sort out some business problems and he'll be away all day. He's told me to entertain you in his absence, if that's all right?' She helped herself to a huge bowlful of fruit as she chatted, her manner relaxed.

Obviously Gerard hadn't confided their difficulties to his sister, Kit thought warily, but then he probably looked on her as a transient house guest who would soon be gone after barely causing a ripple in their well-ordered lives. That being the case, why should he even bother to mention her to Colette? The thought was incredibly depressing, but her concern for Halima, which had been present since awakening, was stronger, and now she seized the opportunity while Colette was by herself to speak to her about it.

'Colette?' She reached for the coffee-pot, forcing herself to appear cool and relaxed. 'Halima had a big bruise on her face yesterday. Do you know how it happened?'

'Did she?' Colette looked up in surprise. 'Well, she was fine in the evening before you came back although her youngest had been playing up a little, stomach-ache I think. Perhaps she fell?'

'That's what she said.' Kit looked straight into Colette's lovely green eyes. 'But I don't believe her.'

'Don't you?' Colette's surprise deepened. 'Why on earth not? Surely she wouldn't lie about something like that? An accident is an accident, after all.'

'If it was an accident,' Kit said grimly.

'What do you mean?' Colette straightened in her seat, spoon poised midway to her mouth. 'Are you saying someone hurt her? But that's ridiculous, who?'

'You say she was all right earlier?' Kit asked slowly.

'Absolutely fine.' Colette nodded positively. 'I had an early dinner, cold meat and salad as we didn't know what time you and Gerard would be back, and then Claude called to pick me up. She was fine then, absolutely fine.'

And then she had come home with Gerard. And they had argued. And he had been white with rage. But he wouldn't. He wouldn't, would he? She shook away the black thoughts, unable to face what she was thinking. 'Perhaps she did fall, then.' She forced a strained smile and reached for her cup. 'She must have.'

The two women spent the day in the shady comfort of the courtyard, alternating between spurts of conversation and long lazy silences. Colette was easy to be with, Kit discovered, the very antithesis of Gerard in fact, and she found herself warming to his sister with each hour that passed. The mood of relaxed serenity came to an abrupt end after a phone call to Colette towards evening time.

'That was Gerard.' Colette smiled as she walked back to the two sun-loungers set under the dappled shade of a huge African fern. 'He had lunch with Claude apparently, and has offered to take us all out tonight. We're to be ready for seven.'

'Oh.' Kit stared at her as a little thrill of apprehension reared its head. Was it coincidence that Gerard had had lunch with Colette's fiancé or did he think that by inviting the other two along she would find it impossible to refuse to accompany him? 'Does he often lunch with Claude?'

'Fairly often,' Colette said blithely as she settled herself comfortably on the warm lounger. 'They do a lot of business together; it was through Gerard that I met Claude.'

'I see.' So this could well be a business angle and nothing to do with her at all. She shook herself mentally for letting her imagination run away with her. She should have known she wasn't that important to him after all.

'Gerard asked if you'd remembered anything. You haven't, have you?' The lovely green eyes glanced her way as Kit shook her head slowly.

'No, not really, just the odd thought that comes and goes.'

'Right.' Colette nodded as she settled herself back and shut her eyes. 'Well, ten more minutes and then I guess we'd better get ready. The restaurant Gerard mentioned is an old Moorish palace and there's a good floor show. It's mainly for the tourists of course, but the folk dancing and music is excellent and Gerard thought you might like it.'

Colette meant nothing by it, Kit knew that, but somehow the other girl's words emphasised her fleeting, transitory influence in their lives more than anything else could have done. She *was* just a tourist after all, she told herself bleakly, and an incompetent if not downright pathetic one at that. What would have happened to her if Gerard hadn't stepped in and taken over as he had? She felt a little trickle of icy foreboding run down her spine in spite of the warmth of the day. And what would happen to her now he had?

She found it difficult consciously to titivate her appearance as she got ready for dinner later that evening. Somehow making the best of herself didn't come naturally at all and she wondered why, applying just a light touch of brown eye-shadow on her eyelids and a touch of mascara on the long thick lashes that shaded her eyes, and then feeling distinctly uneasy at the effect as her eyes widened and darkened, turning into luminous black pools. She was just thinking about washing the make-up off and keeping her skin bare of all embellishment as usual when Colette entered the room after a cursory knock.

'Nearly ready?' The other girl was stunning in a black catsuit of raw silk that showed her lithe, neat body off to perfection, the copper hair loose and flowing in soft curls and waves to her shoulders and her eyes outlined in a vivid green that should have looked outragreous and didn't. 'Aren't you going to wear any make-up?'

'I have.' Kit motioned to her eyes awkwardly. 'But I think I'll wash it off, it doesn't suit me.'

'Rubbish.' Just for a second the likeness to Gerard was overwhelming. 'You could get away with heaps more with that short bob, it emphasises your marvellous bone-structure and lovely eyes, but you don't make the most of them. Here...' She took a make-up brush from the dressing-table and dipped it in a pot of pearly powder carefully. 'Just the barest touch across your cheekbones to highlight them.' She stood back to admire the effect, her eyes narrowed. 'And a little more eyeshadow with just a touch underneath your eyes too. Try this lipstick—I think dark plum is your colour.'

Before Kit could object to the new face staring back at her, a disturbingly beautiful face, Colette's eyes moved to the dress Kit had chosen for the evening that was lying across the bed, a subdued little number in pale grey cotton with long sleeves and a modest neckline. 'You aren't going to wear that?' The other girl's eyes were frankly horrified.

'Isn't it right for where we're going?' Kit asked anxiously.

'No way.' Colette dismissed the dress with a disgusted wave of her hand. 'That's fine for lunch in town but this is an evening out, for goodness' sake. I know just the thing!' She reappeared from the walk-in wardrobe a moment later with a short crimson cocktail dress in crushed velvet, the dark wine material throwing Kit's bare neck and arms into pale relief as Colette held the dress against her chest briefly. 'That's your colour, that's definitely your colour,' she said slowly, her voice satisfied. 'Look what it does to your hair. I never knew it had so much red in it.'

'Look, I don't think——'

Colette waved her objections away without even speaking as she handed Kit the dress. 'Put it on.' As Kit hesitated Colette glanced at her watch. 'We're late, Kit, put it *on*.'

'But——'

'No buts.' Colette's eyes narrowed again when the sleeveless dress was in place, the rounded neck wonderfully flattering against Kit's flawless creamy skin. 'You want something . . . I know.' She raced out of the room only to return thirty seconds later with a long pair of lacy gold earrings in her hand. 'Take those studs out of your ears and put these on,' she said commandingly before stepping back, her head on one side, to admire the overall effect. 'You look stunning.' She shook her head slowly. 'Gerard's going to blow a fuse.'

'Colette!' But Kit was laughing, a sudden feeling of recklessness pervading her whole system. She'd be gone from this place soon and would never see him again. Maybe, just maybe, he might remember her as she looked now if he ever thought about her at all? And somehow, although she knew it was crazy, pointless, it was suddenly desperately important that he did think of her now and again.

'Come on.' Colette took her arm firmly as they left the bedroom as though sensing her nervousness. 'Claude's waiting downstairs. Gerard got delayed with some important business deal but he's home now and will be down shortly.'

He was down already. Both men were sitting waiting in the huge hall as the two women descended the stairs, and as Gerard glanced up and saw her the expression on his handsome face stopped Kit's heart. She glanced away from the naked wonder, the hot and hungry desire that had lit the cold aristocratic face from within, with a feeling of panic gripping her throat. She shouldn't have dressed up, shouldn't have let Colette experiment like this. She didn't want to attract him, she didn't want him to want her, she didn't...

'Kit.' She raised her eyes helplessly to the brilliant gold of his. 'You have taken my breath away.' He wasn't smiling. 'You look quite beautiful.'

'She was going to wear an old grey thing.' Colette was prattling away at her side as Claude moved forward waiting to be introduced, but Gerard seemed blind and deaf to anyone else, his eyes fixed on her hot face as he moved to take her arm in his. 'But that looks so much better, don't you think?' She nudged Gerard sharply as he still didn't speak. 'Are you going to introduce Claude to Kit, then?'

'Of course.' Suddenly the fire was banked down as he noticed the frantic thudding of her pulse against the creamy smoothness of her skin, the alarm she was trying to hide. 'How remiss of me.'

It took the taxi fifteen minutes to reach the restaurant where Gerard had booked the meal and for the whole time Kit was as tense as a bowstring. Gerard was devastatingly cool and enigmatic in an expertly cut light grey suit which, when teamed with the old gold silk shirt and tie he wore so casually, seemed to accentuate the broad shoulders and hard-planed muscled body until she could hardly breathe. She glanced at him under her eyelashes as they passed through an open gate into an avenue of orange trees, geraniums and datura towards a massive building in the distance. The air of authority, of command, was starkly clear even when as now he was relaxed and informal, and it unnerved her. She took a long deep hidden breath. More than a little. She didn't like his strength and power and arrogant masculinity, she found it threatening. She blinked as the cool gaze turned to her, trying to veil her eyes from that razor-sharp male mind.

'You are very thoughtful.' The light, easy tone would have sounded mildly teasing to anyone else, but there was something burning deep in the light brown gaze that told her he had sensed her animosity and was annoyed by it.

'Not really.' She turned her gaze out of the window, glad of the other two's presence in the car. 'Is this the restaurant?' she asked carefully, her voice bland.

'Yes.' As the taxi stopped at the foot of high marbled steps and they alighted into the warm, fragrant night air, Gerard took her arm, slipping it through his before she could object. 'You're with me.' His voice was very low and soft in her ear. 'Whether you like it or not, OK?'

'I don't know what you mean.' She tried to swing round to face him but his arm tightened like steel, forcing her to remain at his side.

'You know exactly what I mean,' he said, still in the same low voice. 'He is in England and I am here and I'm damned if I will play second fiddle tonight. You are with me, Kit. Reconcile yourself to the fact.' There was a coldness in his voice that chilled her blood, but the next moment the other two had joined them and they walked up the steps as an apparently relaxed and animated foursome, although his grip on her arm felt as though it was crushing her bones.

The old palace was in Andalusian style, built round a patio crowded with fountains and plants, and once through the door they walked along a passageway lined with ancient wooden doors behind which the noise and activity suggested the interiors had been made into one gigantic kitchen. The actual restaurant was on the first floor in what had obviously been the main reception-room in years gone by, its mellowed walls lined with weapons below cedar-wood lintels carved with Kufic script and a pine-cone design, and although the vast room was already nearly full the whole atmosphere was one of relaxed benevolence and airy space. One panel at the far end of the room was hung with Berber carpets from the Middle and High Atlas mountains, the predominant colours of dark red and gold giving life and brightness to balance the other, more sombre, walls. The main central part of the huge wall that overlooked the plant-filled patio was a line of delicate stucco arches, the upper portions open to the air and light and the bottom patterned glass, and it was to a table in this prime position that Gerard led them, the waiter bobbing along at his side.

'Would you like me to order for you?' Gerard asked quietly a moment or two later as she stared nonplussed at the menu written in several languages, not one of which was English.

'Please.' She looked up to smile her thanks but saw he was looking elsewhere, the gold gaze trained on a party of eight or more people who had just entered the restaurant at the far end of the room. Almost as though his presence drew her glance, one woman, a little taller and certainly more extravagantly beautiful than the rest, turned her dark head their way, the lovely almond-shaped eyes widening and brightening as she caught sight of Gerard. She raised one slim arm in acknowledgement of Gerard's nod before following the others to a table on the other side of the room, turning her head once or twice more in their direction before she was finally seated.

'Some friends of ours,' Gerard explained briefly as his narrowed eyes returned abruptly to Kit's purposely blank face. She was saved the necessity of a reply by Colette waving to the group in her turn before turning and giving Kit a little breakdown on each one.

'And the woman in the green dress is Zita,' Colette finished quietly as her gaze rested on the siren who had waved to Gerard. 'She'll probably come over in a minute.'

'Guaranteed.' Claude's voice was dry. Gerard said nothing, his eyes veiled and distant as they met hers. Kit didn't ask why, she had the feeling she already knew.

Sure enough, within five minutes Zita arrived at their table and with a sinking heart Kit saw the other woman was even more beautiful close to. Black almond-shaped eyes set in a pearly smooth skin, full red lips that reposed in an inviting pout, long sleek black hair coiled into an elegant braid on the top of her head... She really was something. And her figure! High full breasts, tiny waist and the longest legs Kit had ever seen off a racehorse. 'Gerard...' The perfect lips smiled alluringly. '*Comment vas-tu*?' And she spoke French. Kit almost shut her eyes in desperation. She should have known.

'I am fine, Zita.' Gerard and Claude had stood up at her approach and he now indicated Kit with a wave of his hand. 'This is Kit, who is staying at Del Mahari at the moment. Kit, meet Zita.'

'How do you do?' Even as Kit spoke she knew the relationship between them. The way Zita's smooth slender hand rested possessively on Gerard's arm, the faintly whimsical twist to the beautiful mouth, the way her body inclined just the slightest towards his... The body language said it all. They had been, or were, intimate. There could be no doubt about it.

'This is nice, that you stay with Gerard? You are on the holiday perhaps?' The words were polite and spoken in a husky, heavily accented voice that was pure magic to any man within earshot.

'Yes.' Kit found she could smile quite naturally and talk easily even as her mind functioned on a different plane altogether. It was almost as though she was used to saying one thing and thinking another. 'But I'll be leaving shortly.'

'This is sad.' Zita didn't look sad, Kit thought tightly. In fact the black eyes had lit up at the knowledge. 'You maybe come back again?'

'I doubt it.' As the other woman nodded graciously and turned to speak briefly with Colette and Claude before weaving her way back through the tables, Kit found her hands were clenched into tight fists under the table and forced herself to ease her fingers loose, stroking the tightness out of her knuckles slowly.

'She's very beautiful.' She spoke to the table generally but it was Colette who replied, Gerard sitting in silence, his narrowed eyes watching her every expression.

'Yes, brains as well as beauty too. She's a doctor, a good one I understand.'

'Oh, yes?' Don't react, don't show any feeling at all, she told herself grimly as her stomach turned over. 'Have you known her long?' she asked calmly.

'We grew up together.' Now it was Gerard who spoke. 'Her parents were great friends of mine.' He smiled a cool smile. 'I understand we were inseparable until school age. Zita was sent away to a private school in Switzerland and then university, after which she carved out a first-class career.'

As the waiter appeared at their table the talk turned to food but, although Kit continued to chat and socialise normally, inside she felt raw. And she had thought her pathetic little display tonight would make him remember her? Her mouth twisted bitterly. With women like that around? She was a fool, such a fool. Why hadn't she dressed as she had wanted to tonight? At least then she wouldn't be feeling quite so much like a fish out of water.

The meal was delicious, course after course including Morocco's national dish, *couscous*, moistened by a thin piquant sauce that was quite mouth-watering, but Kit could have been eating sawdust for all it registered on her taste-buds. She was aware of each movement Zita made, every time she glanced over in their direction, her black eyes languorous and warm as they lingered on Gerard's face in profile to her. Gerard seemed oblivious of the other woman's attention as he chatted lazily, his dry wit and cynical repartee drawing many a chuckle from Claude and laughter from the women, although Kit had never felt less like laughing. And he knew she was acting. She glanced at him once as she smiled dutifully at some pleasantry. The gold eyes were icy.

The floor show began as they were eating dessert and Kit had to admit it was breathtaking, from the beautifully dressed folk dancers in their robes of gold and red to the acrobats who whirled and twisted in an incredibly small space without putting a foot wrong. She tried to concentrate, reminding herself that soon all this would be a distant memory, but the sense of outrage and hurt was growing stronger although she was at a loss to understand why. She had no right to feel anything at all where he was concerned. She was engaged to be married, for goodness' sake, and his liaisons were his own affair. He wasn't flirting with Zita, in fact after that first acknowledgement he hadn't glanced at her once, so there was no justification for this bitterness that was filling her mouth with bile. But it didn't help. All the cold logic didn't help.

They sat drinking the thick black coffee the Moroccans favoured as the floor show finished and the space was cleared for dancing. A small band of three musicians appeared to one side of the floor, and almost the moment they began playing Zita and a tall dark-haired man who was obviously her partner for the evening made their way across the room to their side. He was very handsome, Kit noted dispassionately as the two drew near, tall, muscular, with the sort of Eastern good looks that sent European women wild.

'I would like you to meet Salem.' Zita was speaking directly to Gerard as she stood with her hand slipped casually through the other man's arm. 'He's a consultant at the hospital.'

She wants him to be jealous, Kit thought numbly. It was obvious, so obvious that as Kit turned slightly and caught Claude's eye he winked very slowly and then shrugged, his eyes wicked. She smiled back in return, betraying none of the emotion that was twisting her insides into a coiled spring, and watched Gerard as he rose to shake hands gravely with the other man, his face pleasant but reserved. As they all began to chat generally, Zita somehow managed to be leaning lightly against Gerard's shoulder, her high full breasts pressed against his body and a few inches of space between her and Salem now. If Salem noticed the manoeuvre he didn't seem to mind and after a few, and to Kit excruciatingly long, minutes had crept by he surprised her by leaning forward and taking her hand in his.

'Kit? This is a very unusual name.' He smiled, showing strong white teeth. 'Would you care to dance?'

'What a good idea.' Zita's swift response had Kit thinking all this was pre-arranged. 'You dance with me, Gerard, yes?'

'Kit has not been well; I don't think——'

She interrupted Gerard's voice with her own, hurt pride making her eyes brilliant as she rose. Let him dance with Zita, let him do anything he wanted to! She didn't care, she did *not* care.

'I'd love to.' As Salem's hand centred in the small of her back and they began to walk to the dance floor she was conscious of the other two following them a step or two behind, hearing Zita's low throaty giggle with a tightening of every muscle in her body.

One or two other couples had already taken the floor, and as they reached the small raised area the tempo of music changed from a lively beat sound to a soft dreamy ballad. Salem was very circumspect, holding her close but not too close and engaging in conversation as they drifted round. In any other circumstances she might have been bowled over by him, she reflected silently as she smiled up into his undeniably handsome face, but with Zita draped over Gerard like some sort of fur collar just a yard or two away the only emotion she was feeling was one of pure undiluted rage. Zita's dress was cut just low enough to show off her ample bosom to its full advantage while still remaining in the bounds of propriety, and her smooth brown arms were linked round Gerard's neck in a way that reaffirmed all Kit's earlier suspicions. They knew each other well, very well.

'Have you known Gerard long?' Salem was still valiantly trying to pretend that the situation was normal, but as her eyes left the other couple and returned to his she saw his own had darkened, whether with anger or hurt she wasn't sure.

'No, just a week or so.' She forced a polite smile to her stiff lips as Zita's throaty giggle snaked back to them again. 'Have you known Zita long?'

'Too long.' The answer wasn't quite what she expected, and as she raised enquiring eyebrows he smiled with more than a touch of bitterness. 'I've always been around, you know? Like the little puppy accepting crumbs from the rich man's table? I think tonight was the first time I understood why I have been allowed into her bed but not her heart.'

His frankness left her struggling for an appropriate reply, and as he glanced down into her troubled face his own softened slightly, a wry smile touching the corners of his hard firm mouth. 'I am sorry, English Kit, that was not fair. The problem is mine and not yours. I think your Gerard is very fond of you.'

'Do you?' She raised disbelieving eyebrows and now it was her face that was bitter. 'Let's put it this way: if you could have me or Zita, would there be any contest?'

He stopped dead, staring at her for endless seconds before drawing her more closely against him, his chin resting in the soft silk of her hair. She caught sight of Gerard's face for one moment and the expression darkening his countenance brought momentary, if acrid, satisfaction. 'Yes, there would,' he said softly, 'and your Gerard is no fool. You do not trust him?'

'Trust him?' She drew back slightly and rested her hands on his broad chest as she stared up into the hard male face. Zita was a fool. This was a good man. 'No, I don't suppose I do.' She shook her head slightly as the ballad finished. 'Could we go back to our table? I need to powder my nose.'

'Of course.' As they passed the other couple Zita had pulled Gerard's head down to meet hers as she whispered something in his ear, and the hot acid rage that flooded Kit's system enabled her to march through the tables and collect her bag from under her seat on legs that were rock-steady. She was out of the massive arched doorway at the opposite end of the room to the entrance before Colette could offer to join her, but rather than enter the ladies' powder-room at one side of the winding iron staircase she ran down the narrow steps and out into the dimly lit patio they had overlooked from their table during dinner, where one or two couples were sitting quietly enjoying an after-dinner drink in the unusually beautiful surroundings.

She found a quiet spot and sank down on to a convenient, beautifully carved stone seat beside a sparkling fountain, her thoughts in turmoil. She had to be quiet and think. She needed——

'Kit?' She heard Gerard's cool voice with a feeling of doom. She didn't want to talk to him now when she was angry and hurt and working purely on emotion. She needed to get control of herself, probe why Zita's behaviour had upset her so badly. 'Is anything wrong?'

'Wrong?' She smiled brightly, her voice brittle. 'Why should there be anything wrong, Gerard?'

'That is what I am asking you.' He sat down beside her, stretching his long legs out in front of him and leaning back against the stone seat with a hard sigh. 'Why have you come out here?'

'Because I wanted to.' The rage was taking over now, which was the last thing she wanted, but he was so damn cool, so aloof, so detached. 'I wasn't aware I had to ask your permission.'

'Then that was your first mistake.' The arrogant audacity brought her head snapping up to meet his, her eyes glittering with fury. 'I am responsible for your welfare and you are not... well at the moment.'

'I am perfectly well.' She glared at him angrily. 'If you mean I can't remember anything, then say so.'

'All right.' His voice was sharper now. 'That is exactly what I mean. I made myself accountable for your safety and until you are yourself——'

'Myself?' she hissed savagely with a bitter little laugh. 'I wouldn't recognise what "myself" is if it rose up and bit me! But a temporary loss of memory doesn't make me a complete idiot into the bargain.'

'Meaning?' he asked coldly, his voice dry.

'Meaning you and Florence Nightingale in there,' she bit back tightly. 'I would have thought even you would have more sensitivity than to bring me here knowing she'd be around. What are you looking for anyway, a harem?'

'Even me?' He ignored the rest of the accusation as his mouth thinned and the gold-brown eyes narrowed into dark slits.

'Yes, even you.' She was facing him now, half turned on the seat with her body bent slightly forward as though she were preparing to pounce. 'Deny it. Deny you've slept with her.'

'Why would I do a thing like that?' In contrast to her flushed face and burning rage he was icy cool, a veritable block of stone.

'You have, then, you admit it?' She felt the blood in her veins run cold.

'It's not something I have to "admit",' he said with frosty contempt. 'Zita and I were more than friends once, a long time ago, but it is in the past and no concern of yours. Nothing can be gained from pursuing this conversation, so I suggest we return to the others and, just to set the record straight, I had no idea Zita and Salem would be here tonight.'

'Really!' The word was tantamount to calling him a liar, and now he gripped her arm tightly as he jerked her to her feet, his eyes murderous.

'Yes, really. Now if you are finished we will return.'

'Let go of me, Gerard,' she hissed quietly, her voice trembling with outrage. 'I won't be man-handled by you. You might get away with it with those unfortunate enough to have to put up with it, like Halima, but not——'

'I beg your pardon?' She realised too late what the little demon of jealousy had led her to. How could she have said that? she thought in stunned terror, the look on his face draining her anger and leaving her barely able to stand. 'Explain yourself.'

'I didn't mean...' Her voice faded as she searched desperately for a way of escape, but there was none.

'Colette told me of your conversation this morning,' he said icily as he slowly, and very pointedly, removed his hand from her arm. 'Do I take it you have decided that I am the perpetrator of Halima's misfortune?'

There was nothing she could say. She didn't believe it, not really, but the words had been a weapon that she had used to deadly effect and she wished with all her heart that she could have revoked them. It had been cruel and vicious and she was disgusted with herself, but seeing him with Zita like that had done something to her she would never have believed. But that was no excuse. She could offer him no excuse. She stared at him dumbly, her eyes enormous in the whiteness of her face.

'Right at this moment I would like to whip you to within an inch of your life,' he said brutally, his voice harsh and his face bitter, 'but that would only give credibility to the low opinion you have of me. For what it's worth, I have never raised a hand in anger to any woman in my life and quite honestly I do not care if you believe that or not.' He drew himself up and away from her as though she were untouchable. 'And no doubt you do not.' Dark angry colour had flared across the high cheekbones, the tawny brown hair and gold eyes alive and glowing from the muted light overhead that threw the contours of his face into savage shadow. 'Hell . . .' His eyes raked her ferociously like a furious wild animal about to strike. 'What the hell am I bothering for, anyway? I don't need this.'

'Gerard, I'm sorry. I didn't mean——'

He cut off her voice with a savage gesture of his hand, his eyes glittering with fire. 'You are sorry? *Sorry*?' He gave a harsh bark of a laugh that caused her to flinch. 'Till when? Till the next time? Do you think I am not aware that every time I reach for you you cower away like a frightened doe? Every time I look at you those big grey eyes are wary and afraid with something approaching hate darkening their depths——'

'No!' She shook her head desperately. 'I don't hate you.'

'Yes, you do.' He nodded wearily. 'The more so because of this attraction between us that you do not like but cannot control. There is something in me that you cannot tolerate, Kit, you know it.' She stared at him dumbly, shocked by his perceptiveness. 'You imagine that I can ill-treat Halima, behave like some sort of monster in private and then put on another face for the world. That is it, isn't it, Kit? You do not trust me at all. Well? Do you?' She couldn't answer, her head whirling and her stomach churning as she tried to formulate the confused darkness inside her. She didn't feel like that about him and yet... and yet she did. It was almost as though something was warning her, threatening her every time she was with him and yet she wanted, needed, to be with him too. It was crazy, mad. If she couldn't explain it to herself, how could she possibly expect him to understand?

'I thought I could make you understand if you came to Del Mahari, that with time you would see——' He stopped abruptly.

'See?' she asked brokenly.

'It doesn't matter.' He stared at her bitterly. 'This revulsion, hate that you have for me is too deep, too fierce.'

'You want me to leave?' She forced the words out through the blockage in her throat and it was only as she spoke that she realised how much she wanted to stay, and the depth of her desire was frightening. 'I can go tomorrow.'

'You will stay until I return to Casablanca in a week's time,' he said icily and as he withdrew from her both in body and spirit she realised he had misunderstood her words, that he had thought she was asking to go.

This wasn't about Zita. As she continued to sit in the quiet of the beautiful surroundings, the lap of water from the fountain murmuring in the softness, she struggled to make some sense of the torment. Zita had merely been the catalyst in letting the poison out, but the results had been devastating. He was finished with her, the cold emptiness in those narrow gold eyes had said it all. She might be leaving in a week's time but as far as he was concerned the farewells had already been said.

CHAPTER SEVEN

THE rest of the evening and the drive back to Del Mahari was an unmitigated nightmare from which there was no awakening. Once back at the house Kit disappeared to her room after a cursory goodnight to a clearly troubled Colette and her icily silent brother, reliving the whole disastrous night over and over again in her mind as she prepared for bed until she thought she would go mad.

Zita's party had left shortly after her return to the restaurant to go on to a party of one of the hospital staff, to which Zita had invited them and Gerard had grimly refused. For the remainder of the evening she and Gerard had sat in a sharp splintered silence watching Colette and Claude wound round each other on the dance floor. She had made one attempt to talk to him and had been rebuffed so savagely that she hadn't tried again.

After an hour of tossing and turning and ranting and raving against herself, him and the whole of life in general, she acknowledged defeat and decided to creep downstairs in search of a hot drink. She knew where the kitchen was, although as yet she had not entered it, but with the rest of the household asleep she decided that a mug of warm milk and a quiet seat in the cool of the shadowed courtyard were just what her bruised mind needed. She couldn't stay in her room alone for one more minute anyway; the goblins of fear and panic and regret were going to send her hysterical if she didn't break their vicious circle.

Pulling a light robe over her wafer-thin nightie, she opened the door warily, peering out into the silent landing beyond for a moment before treading quietly across the stained wooden floor and walking to the top of the stairs. The house was eerily unfamiliar in the grey gloom of the night, but such was her despair and hopelessness that she could have been confronted by the devil himself and not turned a hair. The ache in her chest was a physical pain that took her breath away, compounded of so many emotions that she would have found it impossible to name just one.

On reaching the ground floor she found the kitchen without difficulty and made herself a warm drink from the cartons of goat's milk in the massive, sparkling clean refrigerator. Before she left, she glanced round the enormous immaculate room which was filled with every modern convenience known to man. He was wealthy, enormously, fabulously wealthy and handsome, successful, intelligent into the bargain. She supposed she ought to feel flattered that he had noticed her at all in the biological sense even if it was as a temporary diversion, but she didn't. She felt crushed and wretched and more alone than she had ever dreamt it was possible to feel.

'You are *not* going to cry,' she told herself fiercely as the rush of tears at the back of her lids made her eyes sting. 'You are going to get over this, find out who you really are and start living the rest of your life. This was just a temporary refuge, he told you that.' She brushed across her eyes angrily with the back of her hand. And this fiancé in England. No one could *make* her marry him if she didn't want to, and she was suddenly absolutely sure she didn't. The knowledge relaxed something deep in her being. Just hearing that petulant male voice on the telephone had told her that.

She had just padded silently down the steps into the courtyard, making for a low wooden bench seat built in a circular design round one of the largest fountains, when a slight movement on the periphery of her vision brought her heart thudding into her mouth. She froze, moving silently into the shadows as she peered through the semi-gloom of the warm tropical night, acutely aware of her lack of clothing.

'Convince me I am not as drunk as I would like to be and you are not an apparition.' Gerard's voice didn't sound at all intoxicated. In fact it sounded lazy, sardonic and full of a derisive cool mockery that seared into her tissues like fire considering the circumstances. How dared he be so in control, so off-hand, so damn *imperturbable* when she was falling apart? None of this had really affected him at all. He wasn't real, he just wasn't real.

'I didn't think anyone would still be up,' she said tightly without moving, pulling the robe more firmly over her breasts with her free hand.

'Oh, I am up, Kit. I am definitely up.' He rose from the very seat she had been making for and, as her eyes adjusted to the darkness, she saw a bottle of whisky on the floor, half full, with an empty glass beside it. 'Won't you join me?' He waved one hand in an expansive gesture that made her realise he had changed since they had returned and was dressed in the Arab clothes of that first night. She stood hesitating, half hidden under the protection of an overhanging palm, only to jump violently as his voice stabbed through the air like a knife, all pretence of non-chalance gone. 'I am not going to rape you, woman; there is no need to look at me like that.' He reached her side with a few swift steps and she found she was quite unable to move although every instinct urged flight. 'You obviously came out here to sit,' he said grimly, 'so sit.' There was no way her legs were going to carry her over to the seat he had just vacated, so rather than in-flame him still more she sank down on to a small stone wall enclosing a mass of sweet smelling roses, their perfume heavy in the still night air.

'Do you still want me, Kit, physically I mean?' he asked after a full minute had ticked away in painful scrutiny. He was standing looking down at her from his great height, legs slightly apart and hands on hips for all the world like some powerful sheikh safe in the protection of his own little world where his authority and influence were law. 'You wanted me that day in the mountains, do you remember?'

Did she remember? She prayed that the extent of her wanting wasn't written on her face. 'I don't think this is going to get us anywhere——'

He laughed harshly, sitting down on the wall next to her so the warm spicy male smell of him enveloped her and his thigh was pressed close to hers. She could feel herself begin to tremble as her pulse began jumping like a yo-yo. He was different tonight somehow; it was as though a brake that had always been applied before had suddenly been lifted. 'Well, the softly-softly approach sure as hell didn't win any bouquets, did it?' The bleak, cynical tone of voice hurt her and she turned to look at him to find his eyes narrowed on her face. She tried to veil her gaze but it was too late, she found herself melting into the rich golden brown that circled jet-black centres over which his heavy, thick black lashes curled in an almost feminine display. But there was nothing else feminine about the hard ruthless face staring back at her so arrogantly, it was pure male and infinitely threatening. 'Well?' His square jaw was set ominously. 'You have not answered my question?'

'I . . .' She felt mesmerised by the sensual aura reaching out to entrap her. His eyes were hungry, leaving her in no doubt as to what he wanted, his mouth twisted with an intense craving that found an answering echo in herself. 'Leave me alone——'

'Answer me.' His accent was very pronounced, his voice deep and husky. 'Tell me you do not want me, that you feel nothing when I hold you in my arms, and I will not touch you again, I swear it.'

She could feel the very air around them, each tiny particle thick and heavy with expectation, and somewhere in the undergrowth a tiny cricket sent its unmistakable sound into the night. The electric excitement that was causing her blood to sing through her veins also sent shivers of fear flickering down her spine. He was so big and dark, so alien in his flowing Arab clothes that sat on the muscled frame in a way that sent hot desire coursing through her body until her legs felt weak. How could she feel so attracted and so threatened at the same time? It was as though she were two different people in the same skin, or maybe... The thought froze her breath. Maybe her intuition, her sixth sense, cut through all the layers of civilisation and the guise he showed to the world and recognised something evil underneath?

'I don't want you.' The words were a soft sigh on the perfumed air and they both knew she was lying.

As one powerful arm moved behind her back the other hand lifted her chin imperiously to meet his mouth, but instead of the harsh invasion she was expecting his lips were soothing and light, stroking her mouth and tasting her slowly as he drew her more closely against him. As the kiss deepened and his tongue began to explore the sweet hidden recesses of her mouth, the raw desire that had hit her so savagely before returned with renewed vigour. She forgot she was almost naked, more so as the robe fell open as she arched and moved against him, she forgot everything but the shattering sensation of being in his arms and having him make love to her.

The hand under her chin moved up into her hair, his fingers threading the red silk tightly as he drew her head back for further penetration, and now his tongue was a hungry invasion causing the delicate nerves near the surface of her skin to burn hotly as they became suffused with blood.

His free hand began to move sensuously over her velvet skin, softly, carefully at first and then, as he felt her complete submission, his touch became more intimate until she moaned completely, completely lost in this her first sexual experience. His tongue flicked lower to her throat, detouring to her ears for long breathtaking moments before continuing its descent, his breathing accelerating sharply as he felt her helpless trembling.

She wound her fingers into the crisp richness of his hair, its texture rough and virile under her searching hands, and then he moved to cover her mouth in another sweet, hungry kiss that was unbelievably sensitive for such a big, arrogant giant of a man. And it was the tenderness that was her undoing. As he swept her on with him to each new embrace, each new intimacy, she lost the power of rational thought. The world and everything in it consisted of Gerard's touch on her skin, his mouth on hers, the feel and smell of him enveloping her very spirit.

'Come...' As he swept her up in his arms and began to walk with her the dizzy, intoxicating effect of his lovemaking was temporarily curtailed. He had passed through the graceful arch and was walking up the stairs before she could control her breathing enough to speak, and then her voice was a weak whisper against the hardness of his body.

'Gerard?' The narrowed gold eyes glanced down at her, a fire in their depths that caused her heart to pound. 'What are you doing?'

'We will be more comfortable in my room.' He smiled down at her, kissing the tip of her nose as he spoke although she had caught the shakiness in his voice. 'I want this to be slow and perfect, I do not want anything to spoil it. I want to kiss every inch of that satin-smooth skin until you beg for fulfilment. I want it to be right.'

'Gerard——'

'I want you, Kit, but it is more than that, do you understand me?' He stopped at the top of the stairs as he gazed hard into her liquid grey eyes.

'But Zita? And the others...' Cold reason began to quell the fire and soon the trickle was an icy flood. 'I'm not like that, Gerard. I can't just make love with you and then walk away.' She began to struggle panic-stricken in his arms and he held her close for one more moment before letting her feet touch the ground while still keeping her in the circle of his arms.

'Listen to what I am saying to you——'

'No!' She tried to shrink from him but the steely arms were too strong. 'You said that day on the mountains that I would have to want you with my mind as well as my body, and I don't. I don't, do you hear!'

'Why not?' His face had changed, the tender light in his eyes being replaced with a fiery anger that was blazingly hot. 'What the hell do you see when you look at me, anyway?'

What did she see? She stared at him aghast. She saw a man that she wanted without rhyme or reason in the emotion. She saw a man who had unlimited power over both her mind and body and had only to click his fingers for her to fall at his feet. She saw someone who terrified her senseless. Her eyes mirrored both her horrified self-awareness and her shock of the full knowledge of it, but as he searched her face he read only the fear, disgust and blind panic.

'If I walk away from you now it is the finish, *vous comprenez*?' He let go of her and stepped back a pace, the robes swirling round his hard form as he folded his arms and surveyed her with eyes that were as cold as ice, his burnished hair gleaming in the light from the oil lamp left burning halfway down the landing. 'Do you understand me, Kit? I will never reach out to you again. I have stood all I'm going to take and so the decision is yours. I will not carry you into my bed kicking and screaming, dammit——'

'Gerard——'

'No, I will not have this "Gerard, Gerard",' he ground out savagely, his face proud and aloof. 'I want a woman in my bed, not a spoiled child who changes with the wind.'

Her eyes were the wounded eyes of a hunted animal and, as she tried to speak and failed, something pierced his heart and caused a constriction in his chest that made it impossible to breathe. How dared she affect him like this, reduce him to this and still look at him like that? Couldn't she see what she was doing to him? What she had been doing to him since the first damn moment he had laid eyes on her? 'Well?' He didn't know what was driving him on to smash even the remote chance he had of making her trust him a little, let him into that closed mind, but at this last rebuff something had snapped. 'What is it to be?' He watched her drag her eyes from his face and turn slowly, her shoulders stooped like an old, old woman, and as she walked down the landing and into her room, shutting the door quietly, he wondered what he had ever done to suffer agony as he was feeling now.

As the next few days crept by in some sort of terrible normality, Kit found she could just survive if she kept her mind in an empty vacuum. Gerard disappeared into his study every day immediately after breakfast to re-emerge in the evening in time for dinner, his face stony and closed and his body tense. Meal-times were something to be endured, the atmosphere so fraught that she couldn't eat a thing and her nerves stretched to breaking point after an hour in Gerard's grim company. Poor Colette, after the first day, had retreated into a bewildered but polite silence after Gerard had snapped so fiercely at her that her face had gone white with pain and outrage. She clearly didn't understand what was happening but just as clearly wasn't going to get involved, and Kit couldn't blame her. Gerard as he was now was enough to deter anything and anyone.

On the morning of the day she was due to return to Casablanca Kit woke early before it was light and lay for hours watching the sun rise, her mind dull and aching. Gerard had informed her the night before in a terse, short statement that they would be leaving shortly after breakfast, and as Colette was away with Claude's family for the day she had already said her goodbyes to Gerard's sister, who had been quite tearful.

As her mind began to stir itself and begin the torturous cross-examination that she had to stop a hundred times a day, she flung the covers back quickly, diving into the shower and washing her hair before dressing quickly in her own clothes and deciding on a slow walk round the gardens before breakfast. She had to do something to maintain the numbness she had forced her mind into over the last few days, she couldn't break down now.

It was still very early and the air was soft and warm, carrying a faint promise of the heat of the day in its perfumed depths as she crept quietly out of the sleeping house and into the fragrant beauty of the gardens. She wandered for over an hour in the delicately landscaped surroundings, sitting for some time in an exquisitely fashioned bower under the shade of an almond tree watching a host of small birds wash and brush up in a large bird-bath, fighting and squabbling as they pushed for the best position like a group of naughty schoolchildren.

Soon she would be in Casablanca, probably only stopping overnight if a flight home could be arranged for the next day. Home? The word pierced the numbness with brutal clarity. Where and what was home? Who was David, Emma...? When would she *remember* ...? She jumped up as the same old pattern reared itself. She wouldn't think of this now, couldn't, not when the parting from Gerard still had to be faced and overcome. As she walked towards the house she glanced at her watch and realised breakfast would soon be ready, her footsteps quickening as she reached the path near the servants' quarters that led past the kitchen and into the side of the house.

The first piercing cry brought her to a dead stop with her hand clutched to her throat as she listened to the sound being cut off in mid-stream. What or who was that? She stood frozen to the spot, unable to move, as her ears strained to catch more cries. There was absolute silence for a few seconds and then a child's voice began to whimper shrilly, the sound something between a cry and a moan, but with a blood-curdling familiarity that brought the fine body hairs all over her skin standing on end. Then a woman's voice began to wail loudly, joined a moment later by another female shouting, and within seconds the uproar was added to by a man's voice ranting and raving in Arabic, his tone harsh and full of furious anger.

As Kit glanced desperately up and down the deserted pathway wondering if she should venture into the door facing her and interfere in something that was definitely not her business, she was almost knocked off her feet by Amina, who emerged from the arched doorway like a bullet out of a gun. The small Moroccan woman clutched at her arm, her face desperate. '*Minfadlik, minfadlik.*' She gestured into the interior pleadingly as the noise rose.

'Amina?' Kit shook her gently, her face white. 'What is it? I don't understand. Is someone hurt?'

'Please, you come.' Such was Amina's agitation that she was trying to drag Kit towards the open door. 'Come, come now.'

'Amina?' Kit heard Gerard's voice with a feeling of overwhelming relief as the two women turned to see him emerge from the far interior of the house with Assad, obviously having enjoyed an early morning ride. 'Amina, *shnoo hada*?' At the sight of Gerard and her husband Amina burst into noisy sobbing, the flood of Arabic that passed her lips interspersed with a wailing cry that was echoed by the other voice inside the house which she presumed was

Halima's. By the time Gerard reached them his face was black with rage and, after physically placing Amina in Assad's arms with a muttered command in Arabic that Kit didn't understand, he strode past her and into the noise inside, his eyes glittering with unholy fire. A moment or two after he disappeared the noise was cut off as though by a knife and then he reappeared in the doorway with one of Halima's children in his arms, a little girl of about five. As Amina's hands reached instinctively for her niece and he placed the whimpering child into her arms, Kit was shocked to see Gerard's knuckles on his right hand were bruised and bleeding as though he had been in a fight.

'Gerard——?'

'Just a moment.' He spared her a swift glance before conversing with Assad and Amina in their native tongue for some moments, gesturing as he finished towards their quarters, to which they promptly disappeared with their little bundle.

'Gerard?' She touched his arm tentatively, her face white, and as he turned to face her saw his face was contorted with a bitter rage that was frightening.

'The man is an animal.' He shook his head slowly, raking back his mass of tawny brown hair from his forehead and leaving a smear of blood from his bleeding knuckles on the brown skin. 'This time he has gone too far.'

'An animal?' she asked weakly.

'How a creature like Abou can father numerous offspring and yet Assad and Amina are childless beats me,' he continued with savage bitterness, his mouth twisted with anger. 'Well, I warned him the last time I wouldn't stand for any more; this is on his own head. I have shamed him no more than he has shamed himself.'

'Gerard, are you saying that Abou beats his family?' Kit asked faintly as she felt the present begin to recede and a terrible blackness grip her soul. 'Is that it?'

'Of course that's it,' Gerard answered irritably as his eyes searched the empty doorway, an ominous silence from within. 'I would not have the man within a thousand miles of here except for the fact that by employing him his family comes under my protection and Assad and Amina are on hand too. It is unbelievable that Assad came from the same womb that housed that savage.' As his eyes moved back to her they narrowed with alarm at her glazed eyes and chalk-white face. 'Come, do not be so upset. A drink will calm . . .'

Colin. Her stepfather Colin. As her memory returned in a flood of nausea she knew why the sound of Halima's child's screams had shocked her so. They were her screams, her cries, her hurt. For ten long years she had lived in the fear of one man, her mother's second husband. Her own father had died when she was five years old and within months her mother had married again, to a man who was obsessed by his big, voluptuous wife whose selfish, fleshly nature was in perfect harmony with his own lecherous desires. From the first moment Kit had set eyes on him she had feared and loathed him, her hate only being equalled by his for this scrap of puny humanity who took some of his wife's attention from himself. At first her mother had tried to protect her from the beatings, the neglect, the mental cruelty, but the erotic, lascivious world he had introduced her to was too much of a pull and soon she was submissive to every word he said. The gut-wrenching fear and dread that had accompanied every second of Kit's waking hours for years returned in its full horror.

He had been a tall, handsome giant of a man with a synthetic charm that could be turned on at the drop of a hat and his dominating, sensual, arrogant nature had apparently found no fault in her mother whom he had loved to the exclusion of everything and everyone else. The days and weeks and months of time spent locked in her room had been preferable to the spasmodic beatings incurred for any little minor fall from grace, but it was the mental cruelty that had hurt the most. The subtle, and not so subtle, mockery of her thin, boyish shape, the constant ridicule and searing contempt that had marked her childhood and teenage years had left their damage.

When Colin and her mother had been killed in a car accident just after her sixteenth birthday they had left her extremely well off financially and an emotional cripple. Masterful men, especially if they were good-looking, she found quite repellent, preferring males who had no power to touch either her heart or her intellect. She had to be in charge, absolutely and unequivocally, physically and emotionally. That part of it she had never understood till now, she realised numbly. But as the handful of boyfriends that she had had before David flashed across her mind, she saw they were all from the same mould, easily led, happy to take second place, content with the odd chaste kiss and making no demands on her in any way. And she had gone out of her way to make sure she didn't attract the more masculine type of male—the severe hairstyle, lack of make-up, subdued colours... She raised her eyes to Gerard's concerned face. And it had worked. Until now.

'Kitten?' The use of the endearment after days of a formal and cold Kit sent hot panic shooting through every nerve. 'You have remembered, have you not?' He swore softly as he took in her enormous pain-filled eyes and white mouth. 'What is it? What has made you look like this?'

His movement to take her into his arms was one of pure compassion with no sexual undertones at all, but as his flesh touched hers she leapt backwards with such revulsion that his blood ran cold. 'Don't touch me.' Her mind was struggling to accept the enormity of what it had been trying to forget as well as the knowledge that with this man, and with only this man, she had let down the defences. She had allowed him to touch her because she had been unable to fight the attraction that was in every square inch of that big male body, she had allowed him to disturb her, to subdue and subjugate, *she had allowed him into her head*. 'Don't you ever touch me again.'

'You are ill.' Her eyes were dilated, the veins on her forehead standing out in stark contrast to the ghastly pallor of her skin, but as he reached for her again she almost snarled her warning.

'Stay away.' She backed from him in much the same way as one would retreat from a ferocious wild animal. 'You disgust me, do you hear?' As his face turned white, something painful pierced her heart but she forced herself to go on. She had given him too much power; if he but knew, he had it all. What could she do? *What could she do*? She loved him. She had committed herself to the very thing that would destroy her if she didn't tear it out by its roots. 'I never want to see you again.'

And then she ran, blindly and with her heart bursting, until she reached the sanctuary of her room where she collapsed on the floor to lie panting and stunned by the enormity of the confrontation until it was time to walk out of his life forever. And it had to be forever. Her flesh crept as she allowed herself to recall little separate instances from her childhood that had been devastating at the time. Colin had taught her to think of herself as both unlovely and unlovable, discouraging any friends that she might have had and insisting on a rigid regime that had him snarling like a dog if she so much as took a step out of place. She had been petrified most of the time, a fact that still had the power to make her curl up with shame.

And when David had betrayed her...? She took the incident out of the back of her mind and placed it squarely in the light. She had been horrified and upset and disgusted but—— She paused as she forced herself to face the truth. It hadn't touched the part of her she had kept for herself. In a strange kind of way she had hardly expected anything better of him. So why had she allowed herself to become his fiancée in the first place? The answer was stark and clear and brutally ugly. Because he would never be able to have any power over her, she hadn't loved him.

She sat up abruptly and wrapped her arms round her legs, her eyes staring blindly ahead. She had chosen him simply because she didn't love him, because there would never be any danger of her loving him; she could always be in control of her emotions and his influence over her.

And Gerard? Gerard was different. Dangerously, menacingly different. She had survived the years with her stepfather as much because of her hate for him as her will to escape his authority over her and make a new life for herself when she was older. She had vowed he would not break her, that the ultimate victory would be hers. But Gerard could shatter that new life, destroy her peace of mind for evermore if she was foolish enough to let him. Love was stronger than hate, she had always known it really; that was why she had avoided it all her adult life. And love was a luxury she dared not allow herself. The final price might be too high, it could destroy her. Because if he ever got tired of her, rejected her after she had opened up her heart and her body to him, she would not survive it. And how, looking as she did, being the sort of person she was, could it end any other way?

She didn't realise until much later that Colin had won after all.

CHAPTER EIGHT

THE journey to Casablanca forever remained a blur in Kit's mind. She was to recall in later days snatches featuring Gerard, his mouth taut with pain and his eyes stony, dealing with the endless formalities and settling her into her hotel, but at the time the emotional vacuum that had followed the storm of emotion held until the moment he left her at the hotel.

'Kitten?' They were standing in the reception area of the hotel lobby, Gerard having acquired her key for her from the receptionist. She had no luggage and had firmly refused his offer to see her to her room. 'You must tell me what is wrong. Is it David? Did he hurt you in some way?'

As though the name were a magic key she suddenly saw her avenue of escape. He wanted her, physically he wanted her very much, he had made that perfectly plain, and being the sort of man he was he might pursue her if she didn't finish this thing in a way he would understand. 'David?' She forced herself to look up into his face, the first time she had consciously looked at him since the moment her memory had returned, and was shocked to the core by the surge of feeling that flooded her system as she took in his strained face and worried eyes. She loved him, how she loved him. She wanted to wipe away that look of concern in the gold eyes, smooth out the lines at the side of his mouth and eyes—— She caught herself abruptly. This was forbidden territory and dangerously, criminally treacherous. 'Of course David hasn't hurt me; we're engaged to be married, aren't we?'

'Exactly.' His eyes held hers tightly. 'Something is strangling you and he seems the obvious solution.'

'I'm fine.' She shook back a lock of hair from her face, vitally aware that he had been careful not to touch her since the episode with Halima's child, and forced herself to continue. 'And I can assure you I am not worried by David in any sense.' The ring of truth in her words convinced him and the frown that was marring his brow deepened. How could she be worried by a creep like David? she asked herself desperately. Compared to Gerard he was a mere boy. 'I just want to get back to him now,' she continued bleakly as her stomach clenched at the lie. 'See him, hold him—you know how it is.'

'How it is?' He echoed her words in such a mild tone that she was fooled until she glanced up into his face again.

'And you should be pleased,' she continued wildly. 'You can get back to the sort of woman you prefer now. Women like Zita, voluptuous, sexy, real women——'

'To hell with this.' He took her arm in an iron grip that was intensely painful and almost dragged her into the small deserted coffee lounge at the side of reception, forcing her into a seat with scant regard for her feelings in the matter. 'Sit down, shut up and do not move,' he ground out angrily through clenched teeth, his eyes blazing.

Strangely the show of strength, of brute force, did not intimidate her at all, it was almost a relief. He was running true to form like all his type, like Colin. He wanted her and that was all that mattered, this animal desire that had to be sated.

'Don't try to bully me, Gerard,' she said coldly. 'It won't work.'

'Bully you?' He stared at her, his face incredulous. 'Is that what you think I'm doing? Can't you see even now?' He shook his head slowly, his eyes searching her strained face for something, anything.

'Of course that's what you're doing,' she said bleakly, 'what all your type do. At least David——'

'David?' He spat the name into her face with terrifying bitterness. 'Do not hold this David up to me as some sort of hero or I shall not be responsible for my actions. If your fiancé is such a model of virtue, why the hell did he let you travel alone to a foreign country knowing you could not speak a word of the language? Answer me that? And he must have known that something had happened that had terrified you?'

'It's not like that——' She caught herself abruptly. She couldn't explain, either about the circumstances of her coming to Morocco or about her childhood and Colin. No, definitely not that. She had never been able to speak of it to anyone, feeling in some strange, totally illogical way that part of it was her fault. If she had been prettier, nicer, more lovable——

'The hell it isn't.' He reached out and shook her angrily. 'If you were mine I would protect you with my life, not set you up for pot-shots from every Romeo who might try his luck.'

'You have no idea what you are talking about.' His touch, even in these circumstances, had started off a chain reaction in her body that spoke more eloquently than words of how dangerous this man was to her self-control.

'Maybe.' He eyed her grimly. 'And why is that? Because you will not talk to me, *really* talk to me. I know no more about you now than when we first met. *Mon dieu*——' he raked his hair in that gesture she was beginning to know '—can you not see that you are being monstrously unfair to both of us?'

'There is no "us".'

'Oh, yes, there is,' he corrected softly, his eyes as hard as flint. 'There is very definitely an us, kitten, whether you like it or not. Do you want me to prove it to you?' Before she had any idea of his intention he had taken her mouth in a hard, cruel kiss that burnt into her flesh like fire, his lips grindingly hard against hers, his arms rigid bands around her body. She tried to fight him, for long seconds she really tried, and then she melted into his embrace helplessly as his lips worked their sensual magic. When he finally let her go he was breathing heavily, his eyes glittering hotly. 'Well?' His voice was arrogant and she didn't have the experience to recognise the desperate uncertainty it was concealing. 'Can you deny what is between us?'

You are talking about sex, she told him silently as she touched her bruised swollen lips with the tip of a finger. Animal lust, biological attraction, call it what you will. I have seen what that does. There has to be more than that.

'Goodbye, Gerard.' She left the coffee lounge expecting he would follow, call her, something, but it wasn't until she had reached the lift and the doors had closed that she realised she had just said goodbye to him in the final sense.

On reaching her room she found it was all as she had left it, her own clothes neatly packed away in the mirrored sliding wardrobe, her shoes neatly arranged below. Ordered and controlled and safe. Just as she ran her life. She heard the sound of a little animal whimpering and it was a few moments before she realised, with a sickening lurch of panic, that it was her own voice. This wouldn't do. She stared into the dressing-table mirror and tried to wipe the desperation from her eyes. She was in charge of her own life now and managing OK. She would never give that life, the one she had clawed for herself out of the dregs of heartache and suffering, over to a man like him. However much she loved him. And she did. She stared back at the familiar face in the mirror, glad it was her own again. She did love him so much. What was she going to do? She lay back on the bed and hunted for the release of tears but they wouldn't come. What *was* she going to do? How was she going to get through the rest of her life?

Morning came, as it inevitably did, but Kit had not slept at all. At first light she packed her suitcases and then showered and washed her hair, ringing down to Reception to check they had a note of her request for a taxi at ten. Her flight wasn't leaving until two but she just wanted to get to the anonymity of the airport where, surrounded by hundreds of people, she could really be alone.

The thought of breakfast was repugnant but she went down to the dining-room just the same. She hadn't eaten properly for days now and that, coupled with all the emotional stress, was beginning to make her feel distinctly odd.

She had just forced the last piece of toast down, helped on its way by a strong cup of black coffee, when the screech of burning tyres outside the large plate-glass window made her turn and look through the clear glass. Gerard's Ferrari had just negotiated an emergency stop in a clear no-parking zone which he totally ignored as he leapt out of the car and ran up the hotel steps without even locking the door.

'No...' She shut her eyes as she whispered out loud. She couldn't face him again, this was unbearable. As she glanced desperately round the half-full room she considered, for a split-second, disappearing into the ladies' cloakroom and staying there until he had gone, but immediately the futility of the idea dawned on her. She could hardly incarcerate herself there all day, and even if she escaped into the city eventually she would be forced back to the hotel. Knowing him as she did, he would simply wait until she returned and her luggage, money, even her passport were locked in her room. She took a deep breath and stood up on unsteady legs. From the look on his face this wasn't going to be pleasant.

He wasn't in the lobby and she rang for the lift, hoping against hope she could get to her room before he found her and at least avoid making a fool of herself in public. In those tortuous years of childhood and adolescence she had become very adept at hiding her feelings and maintaining a poker face however bruised, physically or mentally, she might be. But somehow, somehow with Gerard that skill learnt so painfully was quite useless.

As the lift doors opened and he stood in front of her, the blood throbbed in her ears so violently that she thought she was going to faint. He obviously thought so too, moving forward quickly and taking her arm in a firm hold as he drew her inside the lift and pressed the button for her floor, ignoring with regal and uncharacteristic rudeness the two businessmen hurrying towards them.

'Good morning, kitten.' He didn't look down at her as he spoke, keeping his eyes on the closed door as the lift took them swiftly upwards, his hand still tight on her arm as though he was afraid she would run if he let go.

'What are you doing here?' she asked faintly through numb lips. The sight, the feel, the smell of him was making her heart pound so jerkily it actually hurt.

'In a moment.' As the lift stopped and the doors slid open they moved into the thickly carpeted corridor and towards her room at the far end before the full reality of it all hit Kit. Then she stopped abruptly, twisting in his hold as she stared straight up into his dark face, her eyes defiant.

'I'm not moving another step and there is no way you are coming in my room,' she stated flatly.

'Rubbish,' he said calmly, bending down and lifting her into his arms to the startled gasp of a middle-aged couple just leaving their room. '*Bonjour*.' He nodded at them grimly as he strode past, walking the length of the corridor and depositing her outside her room with a determined flourish. 'Do I have to search your bag for your key or are you going to be sensible and open the door yourself?' She stared at him warily as her trembling fingers reached inside her handbag and found the cold metal. In spite of the apparent calm dignity he was furiously angry, she knew it. The narrowed gold gaze glanced down at her, his eyes as cold as ice, and she knew she was right.

She tried twice to open the door but her shaking fingers couldn't insert the key in the lock, and at the third try he took the key from her with a hand that was rock-steady and opened the door at once. 'In.' His voice brooked no argument.

She preceded him into the sunlit room and nerved herself to turn and face him.

'Well?' She had aimed at defiance but her voice sounded more pleading than anything else. That fact alone brought her chin up high. She had had years of grovelling to a madman and had vowed long ago she would never be in that position again.

'Why did you let me believe that you were engaged to be married to David?' he asked with deadly reasonableness.

'What?'

'You heard me!' As she shrank back at the low growl, he physically shook himself, taking a deep breath before he spoke again, his voice back in the even moderate tone. 'You broke off your engagement before you even came to Morocco. Now you might have forgotten that at the beginning but not after yesterday. You remembered the whole caboodle yesterday. So——' he eyed her menacingly '—I repeat my question. Why did you let me think you were still committed to someone else?'

'How did you find out?' she whispered slowly. There was no point in denying it. He knew.

'Your little flatmate was worried she hadn't heard from you since big brother talked to you last,' he said with icy sarcasm. 'She was worried he had upset you. She phoned to say that she was disgusted with the way he has handled your... indisposition and couldn't go along with his lies and deceit. It was a most interesting conversation.' The lethal gaze darkened ruthlessly.

'Most informative. Well?' He took a step towards her and she nerved herself not to retreat. 'I want an explanation.'

'It was easier to let you think I was still involved with David,' she said painfully.

'Easier!' Dark colour flared across the high cheekbones turning his eyes into golden points of light. 'Who the hell was it easier for—you? I've suffered the torments of the damned imagining you going back to him.'

'Don't be silly.' Now she did take a step backwards but more so that she didn't fling herself into his arms than anything else. 'We've only known each other a couple of weeks; there's nothing between us.'

'Do not try that line again,' he said bitterly. 'You know how I feel about you, dammit; everyone else does. I've been through hell trying to adjust my more carnal inclinations to the fact that you were looking towards me for protection, for refuge. That you were ill, frightened. I tried to tread carefully, show you my home, my family, build up your trust, but everything I did seemed to force us further apart and all the time I thought you were being faithful to David. Hell!' He swallowed tightly. 'How you must have laughed.'

'It's not like that,' she whispered desperately.

'Then what *is* it like?' he snarled furiously. 'Tell me, open that beautiful lying mouth and tell me. Why did you break off your engagement?'

'Didn't Emma tell you?' she asked painfully.

'No, she wouldn't.' He gestured angrily with his hand. 'She said he had let you down in some way but that you would tell me if you wanted me to know.'

'I found him in bed with someone else,' she said flatly, hearing his sharp intake of breath as she lowered her head so that her hair shielded her hot cheeks.

'The fool.' She felt him make a move towards her and then stop. 'And that's what you were trying to forget? But all men aren't like that, kitten, don't you see——?'

'That's not it! David's not it!' The words exploded out of her like bullets and then she was absolutely still, her eyes fixed on the floor.

'Kitten, you can't just walk out of my life,' he said softly after a full minute had passed. 'You must realise that. I knew the instant I saw you you were mine——'

'Don't say that.' She raised shocked eyes to his. 'This thing, it's just an attraction between us, like you feel for lots of women. It doesn't mean anything; Zita would do just as well——'

'Stop it.' His voice was steely now and full of authority. 'I want you, kitten, but not just for a day or a week or a year. I want you as my wife, as *mine*, do you hear? I want to share every new morning with you, be there with you at night——'

'No!' If he had suggested a gross obscenity she couldn't have reacted more violently. 'You don't really care like that, you're lying.' Her voice was wild, her eyes desperate. 'Admit it——'

'You don't want me to love you, do you?' His voice was quiet now and threaded with incredulity. 'That is what has frightened you all along, is it not? You sensed this feeling between us just as I did and it scares you to death. Why?'

She shook her head helplessly but he moved to her side in one angry stride and grasped her upper arms tightly, shaking her slightly in his rage. 'Oh, no, no more of that. Damn you, you *will* tell me, Kit. I have no intention of letting you go, and to hell with these secrets. I don't care what you've done, what you've been before you met me——'

'It's nothing like that.' She was as white as a sheet. 'But the sort of love you say is between us is dangerous, cruel and dangerous. I know.'

'How can you?' He stood back a pace, his eyes stony. 'You haven't given it a chance so how can you possibly judge? I have known many women in my life, I admit it, but not one of them has touched my soul until you. You are my other half, Kit, like it or not. It would have been easy to let myself drift into a comfortable relationship, marriage, more than once before now but I knew that essential element was missing. I just didn't know what it was until I met you.' The words that he spoke so sincerely were like a funeral bell tolling in her mind.

'I don't want you to love me like that,' she said wildly. 'Don't you see? A love like that leaves no room for anyone else, the world narrows down to two people and how the strongest can make the other feel. And I wouldn't be able to stand up to you, I'd become just like her.'

'Her?' he said quietly. 'Kitten, we are not talking about the same thing——'

'No, we aren't,' she agreed sadly, the bleakness in her face stilling his breath. And then she told him, her voice flat and expressionless as she detailed the years of humiliation and bitter torment, the constant fear that was with her day and night and the dread of hearing her stepfather's footsteps, his voice. She had known no hope, no joy, no peace in her life until they both were dead, and that all in the name of love...

'That was not love, kitten.' His voice was infinitely tender, his face full of such compassion and concern that she wanted to run from the feeling that was bursting forth inside her. She thought she had seen him in all his moods but this gentleness was a thing apart. 'If your stepfather had truly loved your mother it would have encompassed you too. Love is not something that detracts, it is like the amoeba, it divides only to grow and multiply. It is a good thing this Colin is dead.' Now something blazed briefly at the back of his eyes, swiftly veiled. 'After what you have told me he would not have remained long in this world.'

'You couldn't have done anything.' As she had first finished speaking he had moved to take her in his arms but she had avoided his touch sharply, and now he made the same gesture which she again eluded with a twist of her body as she walked across the room. 'No one would have believed you. I tried time and time again but he was so charming you see, so likeable.'

'I would not have wasted time on words.' There was something in his voice that told her he was deadly serious, and again his very arrogance, his strength, his total confidence in himself sent an icy shiver snaking down her spine. These were the qualities that had hurt her as a child; what made him different from Colin? Everything, her heart sang out in reply. Probably very little, her head countered immediately. 'You have not told these things to anyone before?' he asked softly.

'There was no one to tell,' she answered simply.

'David?'

'David!' She laughed shrilly and then caught herself tightly. It would take very little to make her hysterical and she couldn't let go now. 'No, I couldn't have told him,' she said more quietly. 'David, all my other boyfriends, they were just... friends. You know?' She turned to look at him and saw his face was strained and tense, his eyes concentrated on her face. 'I didn't want more than that,' she said flatly. 'Even with David, believe it or not.'

'And now?' The room was very still, the only sound the low hum of the air-conditioning, and for a moment time seemed suspended as he held her gaze.

'I'm sorry.' The words were dragged out of the depths of her. 'I can't...'

'You can,' he said fiercely.

'No.' She shook her head blindly. 'I don't even know you——'

He reached her side, drawing her into his arms even as she struggled against him. 'You only need to know what is between us,' he said thickly, his mouth meeting hers in a scorching kiss that burned her flesh. 'That is all that matters...' She put her hands on his strong upper arms intending to push him away but somehow, somehow her arms slid up round his neck, her fingers lost in his hair as his mouth continued to plunder hers. She loved him, she loved him so much...

His lips roamed over her face, stroking gently against her closed eyelids, her forehead, her throat. His arousal was fierce against the softness of her body and her own inner thighs were aching, throbbing, with a primitive need that she couldn't hide. As he drew her down on to the soft thick carpet she was hardly aware of what she was doing, all the emotional turmoil and physical strain of the last few weeks culminating in a need to be cherished, desired, wanted. His breathing was harsh and ragged as he ran his hands over her slender body, his lips caressing the rapid pulse at her throat before continuing lower as he crouched over her. Tiny tremors began to shake her limbs as sensation after sensation washed across her body in an ever-increasing momentum, his experienced touch working a subtle magic against which she was helpless. She had never known it could be like this, she thought dazedly. She wasn't herself any more, the person she had known for twenty-five years, he had transformed her—— The thought broke through the sensual warm haze like a thunderbolt and she surprised them both as she shot upwards, scrambling away from him in an undignified retreat to sit panting a few feet away, her eyes wild.

'Kitten?' As he saw the panic in her frightened face he could have kicked himself for going too fast. What was the matter with him? he asked himself savagely. She had just told him she had been through hell on earth for ten years of her life and he was going about things like a bull in a china shop. He swore silently. 'What we feel for each other is natural——'

'But that is how *they* were,' she breathed slowly with horrified revulsion as she struggled to her feet. 'He only ever wanted to look at her, be with her, touch her——'

'He was sick.' Gerard's voice was harsh as he cut into the memories. 'You know yourself he was sick. He didn't love your mother, he was obsessed by her. There is a world of difference between the two.'

'Is there?' She stared at him white-faced. 'But how do I know that what I feel for you is love and not obsession? And how do you know?' It wasn't quite the way he had imagined her declaring her feelings for him, but at that moment he was happy to take anything he could get.

'Darling——'

'No.' She faced him stony-eyed. 'You make me feel vulnerable, helpless, exposed——'

'As you do me.' He made no attempt to touch her now. 'It works both ways, this love.'

'Please leave, Gerard.' He straightened slowly, his body stiffening.

'You do not mean that.'

'I mean it.' She walked past him and opened the door. 'I do.'

He knew he could have her. He glanced at her mouth, trembling a little underneath the bravery, at her eyes, haunted and dark, her mouth still bruised and swollen from their lovemaking. Yes. He could have her. But at what cost to them both and especially her fragile equilibrium?

He walked past her and out of the door.

CHAPTER NINE

'I'M SORRY, David, there is really no chance we could get back together again.' As Kit looked at the tall, attractive man in front of her she wondered how on earth she could ever have considered spending the rest of her life with him. The fair, boyish good looks did absolutely nothing for her and when added to the weak, soft mouth and insipid blue eyes . . . She hid an instinctive shudder. He was nothing like Gerard, nothing at all. Her stomach turned over violently and she resolutely blanked the name.

'I don't blame you,' Emma said vehemently at her side, earning a black scowl from her brother which she returned with sisterly fierceness. 'The thing with Virginia was bad enough, but to lead Kit on like that when you knew she was ill and vulnerable, to pretend——'

'Shut up, Em.' Had his voice always had that faint whine in it? Kit asked herself in surprise. Probably. Very probably.

She had been back in England for a few hours, arriving unannounced at the flat to find Emma all alone and touchingly pleased to see her. David had arrived within the hour for dinner, something he had always been in the habit of doing even before they were engaged, and when he had immediately started to reproach her for not letting him know of her intended arrival she had made it quite clear exactly where he stood. He took it surprisingly well, partly because he knew her well enough to know there was no possibility of her changing her mind and also, and, more to the point, because Emma had made it absolutely plain that she was backing Kit one hundred per cent, both with regard to the business the three of them owned and also in a more personal sense. Emma's loyalty had surprised and touched Kit; she hadn't realised how much the other girl cared about her and the knowledge was balm to her sore heart.

David had just left, without dinner, when the phone rang as she was having a bath, forcing herself to relax her aching muscles in the foamy warm water as Emma prepared their meal. She heard her friend answer the phone, speak for a few minutes and then replace the receiver. 'Kit?' Emma called through the partly-open bathroom door. 'That was Gerard. He wanted to make sure you had got home safely.'

'Did he?' She sat bolt upright in the bath, slopping a great wave of water on to the floor, and took a long deep breath to calm her racing heart before she spoke again. 'Fulfilling the last of his host duties, I should think.'

'Umm...' Emma's voice was thoughtful. 'Are you saying the guy isn't interested in you?'

'Not really.' Kit closed her eyes tightly. She didn't need this right now. 'Ships that pass in the night and all that.'

Emma snorted loudly. 'And pigs might fly.' After that meaningful comment Emma left her in peace and from the sounds in the tiny kitchen continued preparing their steak and salad.

He had phoned. The desolation and sick darkness that had been with her ever since leaving Morocco lifted fractionally. What exactly had he said to Emma? She was out of the bath and into silk pyjamas and a loose towelling robe within seconds, padding through to the kitchen in bare feet as she rubbed her wet hair with a towel.

'Did Gerard leave a message?' she asked casually as she poured them both a glass of chilled white wine and then sat on the edge of the kitchen table watching Emma expertly toss a green salad.

'The ship that passed in the night?' Emma asked drily, as she prepared the two juicy steaks sizzling under the grill. 'No.' She darted a quick look at Kit's carefully blank face. 'He just asked if you were home, how you were, that sort of thing.'

'Oh.' The darkness was back again fierce and strong. She should have known and she couldn't blame him really. He had wanted to know that his duties were discharged, that his commitment was over. She still couldn't believe that he had let her go like that—it went against everything she had learned about his dominant, assertive, hard personality—but perhaps in the end he had decided enough was enough? She flinched inwardly. She was a mess, emotionally and mentally. Perhaps he hadn't wanted a complication like her in his life? And if he had forced himself on her? The thought quickened her breath as she recognised that within a few minutes it wouldn't have been rape. But she would have hated him, and herself, afterwards. But he couldn't have known that, she argued weakly. Could he?

'Kit, what's wrong?' She came out of the reverie to find Emma in front of her, her friend's round face troubled. 'I don't want to pry, I know you are a very private person, but we have been friends for years now and if I can help?' And somehow, unbelievably, she found herself telling another human being of the trauma of those first years within twenty-four hours of first mentioning it to Gerard. It was as though the telling of it to him, and his understanding, compassion and complete lack of censure, had opened an avenue of healing she wouldn't have believed possible. And then she told Emma about Gerard, all of it, and as her voice finally trailed to a halt she found Emma was surveying her through frankly incredulous eyes.

'And you let him go?' her friend squeaked in amazement. 'Kit, they don't come gift-wrapped like that very often. Don't let Colin and your mother continue to ruin your life, for goodness' sake. Ring Gerard, do something!'

'I can't.' Kit shook her head slowly. 'I really can't, Emma. I can't explain but I've got a hell of a lot to work through before I'm fit for myself, let alone anyone else.'

'But that means you've lost him,' Emma said weakly.

'I know.' Kit shut her eyes as the desolation grew. 'I can't bear it.' But there was nothing else she could do.

The next few days were a nightmare of struggling to do her share of the work in their tiny business after sleepless nights, forcing herself to eat although even the thought of food was sickening, and generally going through the motions of life while screaming inside. All she could think of was Gerard and the fact that she had thrown away the only chance of happiness she would ever know, and yet... She forced herself to confront the truth. If he were in front of her, right now, she would chicken out again. She knew it.

She rose, dull-eyed and exhausted, on the fourth morning of her return to England to find a small package on the hall table. 'Postman delivered it a minute ago,' Emma informed her casually as she disappeared into the bathroom for a shower, her nonchalant tone belying the look of intense interest that accompanied it. 'Postmark's Morocco...' The bathroom door shut with a martyrish click.

She looked at the bold black writing that covered the small parcel and her nerves jumped. It was his writing. She knew instinctively. She opened the package very carefully.

'To my darling kitten,' and in brackets, 'I can call you that because you cannot tell me not to, being thousands of miles away. I love you, I will always love you. Wear this sometimes and think of me.' Enclosed was a narrow gold bracelet inlaid with tiny diamonds set in the shape of hearts. She sank down on the hall carpet, the bracelet still in her hand, and cried as though her heart would break.

Flowers arrived the next day, five beautiful red roses, the dew still fresh on their perfect leaves, and again an accompanying note. 'A rose for every day we have been apart. Think of me.'

The next day it was a raw silk scarf, similar to one she had admired on Colette, the message on the card tender and romantic and funny. And the following day a tiny kitten, fashioned exquisitely out of crystal. 'I adore you, my sweet love, never doubt it for a minute.' And so it went on. On the days that a gift didn't arrive a letter would, and she grew to look forward to these more than anything else in life.

The tenor of the letters changed from day to day as he wrote describing his life at work, at Del Mahari, his morning rides, his aspirations for the future, his regrets for the past. 'He's courting me,' Kit realised with a little catch in her breath, three weeks after the first gift had arrived. 'All those miles away and he's courting me.'

'Of course he is.' Emma sighed enviously as she glanced at the tiny water-colour of Del Mahari that had arrived in the morning post signed by the artist himself, G. Dumont. 'I told you, Kit, they don't come gift-wrapped like him too often, certainly not round here.' She glanced out of the window at the driving rain that shrouded the morning with its icy spray. 'The first of November. I bet it's a lot warmer where he is.'

Kit nodded bleakly. Anywhere would be warmer if he was there.

In the third week of November, when the post didn't arrive before she went to work one morning, she felt utterly bereft. Perhaps he was tired of this one-sided courtship? Perhaps yesterday's letter was the last one she would ever have from him? She made more mistakes in one morning than she had made in the whole of her working life, and after she had snapped at Emma and David for the umpteenth time she went home in her lunch hour telling herself she needed an hour away from the business. The indescribable rush of relief that flooded her senses as she saw the thick envelope with that familiar writing lying on the mat informed her that she had been lying to herself. In more ways then one. He wasn't a fierce, passionate stranger any longer, he had opened up his heart and his soul to her, trusting her with the very essence of himself. So what was she going to do about it?

The phone call came a few nights later. She had been lying curled in front of the fire, alone for once, reading through a few of his letters. He had sent her a huge fluffy brown teddy-bear that morning with reproachful honey-gold eyes. 'He can keep you warm at night until we can arrange a more satisfactory substitute. Think of me.'

Think of me? She had done nothing else. He filled her days, her nights, her dreams and slowly, subtly, had filled the void in her past, but her sheer dependence on his strength, his consistency, scared her to death. He wasn't like Colin, she could accept that now, but she couldn't bring herself to make that step of faith, to trust him as he obviously demanded she do.

As the phone rang she picked it up automatically, her mind a thousand miles away, and then froze, her heart pounding as his deep rich voice echoed down the line. 'Hello? Could I speak to Kit, please?' The rush of tears into her eyes was blinding and still she couldn't speak. She loved him, she needed him, she didn't know how she was going to get through the rest of her life without him—— 'Kit? Is that you?' he asked softly after a few tense moments had ticked by.

'Yes.' He would never know the effort it cost her to speak. She was shaking so much she could barely hold the phone.

'How are you?' he asked slowly after another long pause.

'Better.' This was awful. Speak to him, say something, she told herself frantically. Thank him for all the gifts, the cards, but most of all the letters, those wonderful, funny, romantic, sexy, thoughtful letters——

'Good.' She heard him take a hard breath and then he spoke again, his voice soft. 'I have some news for you,' he said quietly, 'something I thought you would like to share. Amina is expecting a little one.'

'She is?' In spite of her turmoil she knew a moment's deep joy. 'That's wonderful, but how did it happen——?' She stopped abruptly as she realised what a stupid thing she had just said. 'I mean——'

'I think I know what you mean,' he said steadily, but she caught the throb of amusement he was trying to hide and flushed hotly. 'I took your advice as it happens, talking to Assad, and once a minor problem was cleared it was all systems go. She is only just pregnant but——' he smiled down the phone '—nevertheless very definitely so.'

'That's wonderful,' she repeated, her voice weak.

'You see it is possible to love someone more than life itself and still care about others?' he said softly. 'Love should beget love, kitten, a stone dropped in the pond of life producing endless ripples. You care about Amina and Assad as do I; that does not threaten or diminish what we feel for each other.'

'Gerard——'

'Listen to me,' he said urgently. 'I am not like Colin and you are not like your mother. *Our* children will be living products of our love to be cherished and protected and cared for, do you understand me?'

'Our children?' It was happening too fast, much too fast, she thought as she raised a hand to her throat, her face stricken.

'I am going to ask you one thing, Kit.' His voice was tense now, a note of harshness in its depths. 'Do you see me in your future at all? I know what you've had to go through, what you are still going through, but I need to know that much. I can show you that we're made for each other, wonderfully compatible in bed and out, I can teach you to trust me, to believe in compassion, tenderness, all the normal things you've missed out on, but only if you allow me in.' There was a blank pause and she heard him swear softly into the stillness. 'Dammit, I need something to hang on to, kitten. It might not be fair but it's what I need. I shouldn't be asking you this, I should be maintaining the strong, silent macho approach while I deluge you with flowers and gifts and love-letters——'

'Don't, Gerard.' Somehow he had managed to sound supremely arrogant and childishly humble at the same time, and it was a dangerous combination. She couldn't think when his voice was stroking over her nerves like thick cream. He was asking her to throw away the safety barriers that had been in place for all of her adult life. If he did love her, and still she could hardly believe that a man like him could feel such a powerful emotion for someone like her, but if he did, how could she love him back as he would expect to be loved when she was such an emotional coward? She bit her lip till it drew blood. She was afraid, of commitment, of belonging, of life and love... With all those inhibitions so firmly entrenched she would destroy them both.

'Is that your answer?' His voice was cold now but she didn't realise it was rigid self-control that was making it that way. She couldn't answer him, couldn't speak the death knell to the future, and so she put down the phone without saying a word. 'Like the coward you are,' she whispered silently into the empty room. 'Colin was right, you don't deserve to be loved. You aren't worth anything.'

There were many times over the ensuing days when she thought she wouldn't get through, but somehow she did. All around her Christmas preparations were in full force but she was untouched by it all, a tall slender automaton mechanically going through the motions. She knew Emma was worried about her and tried to reassure her friend now and again, but even that was a perfunctory response and not one from the heart. Her heart was dead. It had begun to die that first morning when it had waited in vain for his letter, and the morning after that, and after that, until she had accepted the inevitable. There would be no more letters.

Emma and David were going home to their parents' house in Hertfordshire for Christmas and, although Emma tried to persuade her to join them right up until the moment she left on Christmas Eve morning, Kit remained adamant. She wanted a quiet Christmas, she assured her friend brightly. A good rest to recharge her batteries. They both knew it was a downright lie but Emma eventually bowed to a will stronger than her own and left, after obtaining a promise from Kit that she would phone her every morning until she got back. 'Just to let me know you're OK,' she said with transparent concern as she lugged her suitcase down the stairs.

'I'm not going to do anything silly, you know, Em.' Kit smiled wryly in spite of her misery. 'I'm a fighter at heart.'

'Are you indeed?' Emma looked up at her from the open doorway into the street as Kit paused on the last step of the stairs. 'Well, you had the knock-out blow a couple of weeks ago so I still want that phone call.'

The small flat seemed desperately empty when she walked back in after waving Emma goodbye.

She cast a desultory eye over some outline sketches she had been working on at home for a new idea in beachwear but couldn't face them, switched the TV on to find rosy-cheeked children singing carols and general good-will to all men on all channels and switched it off again, and eventually curled up in a chair with a book in which she hadn't the faintest interest.

'You are lucky,' she told herself out loud after reading the same page several times and throwing the book down in disgust. The design business was really beginning to take off and the order book was full, David was reconciled to the change in their relationship and the three of them worked exceptionally well together, she was healthy, young, with no financial worries... She bowed her head into her arms and wept and wept...

After a morning of moping around the flat and indulging in morbid self-pity she got thoroughly angry with herself and went for a brisk walk in Hyde Park for most of the afternoon, returning at dusk to a tea of muffins and blueberry jam. She had reconciled herself to the fact that this Christmas had to be endured but the New Year would be better...wouldn't it?

After a long hot bath she settled down on the settee in silk pyjamas and a warm fluffy dressing-gown, deciding she might as well be comfortable in her misery, glancing round the small room, festive with Christmas cards and a tiny tree that Emma had bought, with heavy eyes and an ache in her chest that was a physical reality. She missed him, unbelievably, desperately so. But it was better this way. She would make him miserable with all her baggage from the past, her insecurities, anxieties, her inability to believe and trust in him. This way he could find someone else. Her heart thudded jarringly but she forced herself to think rationally. He had probably found someone else already or maybe Zita was helping him cope with rejection? Whatever, there had been no letters, no contact since that painful phone call, so he had clearly washed his hands of her once and for all. For the first time she admitted to herself how desperately she had needed a short note, a little card, anything to tell her he was thinking of her this Christmas. But there had been nothing. She bit her lip but the tears were already falling and within seconds were a veritable, scalding hot river.

The doorbell brought her head snapping up in horror. Who on earth . . . ? She waited, rubbing her wet eyes with the back of her hand and sniffing helplessly. It rang again, more stridently this time and then again and again. 'Oh, hell.' They weren't going to leave. She caught sight of herself in the tiny hall mirror just before she opened the door, and shut her eyes briefly at the sight. She had never been able to cry prettily at the best of times and this was *not* the best of times.

'Hi.' As the door opened on its chain and she peered warily through the crack she knew for certain her mind had cracked at last. He couldn't be standing there, not really. She wanted him so much, needed him so much that her subconscious had dragged him up to torment her.

'Kitten?' The big dark figure in its black overcoat moved slightly and she leapt back as though it had burnt her, shutting the door with shaking hands. He *was* here. It was him. And what did she look like? She lay back against the door as her heart pounded and the blood sang in her ears. She didn't believe this. As she slid the chain off and opened the door she stood back a pace staring up into his dear, dear face.

'I didn't think you were going to let me in for a minute there.' He smiled but it didn't reach his eyes, and she noticed his mouth was white with strain, his face tense. 'I take it I *can* come in?'

She couldn't speak, her breath was strangled in her throat, but she stood aside waving him in as her eyes devoured him. As he passed, her senses reeled at the familiar smell of his after-shave, the height and breadth of the big body, the tawny brown hair and darkly tanned skin. He was so good-looking, so dangerously good-looking. What on earth did he want with her?

'Kitten?' He turned as she shut the door and tried another smile which had no more success than the first. He was nervous! She stared at him in amazement as the thought crystallised. He couldn't be... but he was. 'I know you are here by yourself and I don't want you spending Christmas alone,' he said softly, his eyes stroking over her damp flushed face and swollen pink-rimmed eyes and narrowing sharply. 'Have you been crying?' This time his voice was more like the old Gerard, direct and compelling and demanding a reply.

'A bit,' she answered shakily as she rubbed at her nose again, desperately trying to brush her hair back from her sticky face. 'I look a mess——'

'You look beautiful.' His voice was gruff and choked with emotion. 'You could never look anything else to me.'

'Gerard——'

'I know, I know.' He raised his hand in an abrupt acknowledgement of her voice as he swung round to face the window, his back rigid. 'I haven't come here to bully you, kitten, please believe that. I know you need time and I can see that I was trying too hard, not giving you time to think or sort out what you want. It was all me, me, me, wasn't it?' He shook his head slowly, still with his back turned to her. 'I was overwhelming you when you needed desperately to be able to step back a pace and evaluate both the past and present and get it all straight in your head. It was just that I thought I might lose you.' His voice broke but he recovered instantly. 'I thought that when you had sorted it all out I might not feature in your plans and so I was trying to force the pace. I didn't realise it until I phoned you. I'd been trying to reassure you, you see, show you what I am inside, how I think, feel——'

'Gerard.' This time her voice caught him and he turned to face her, his eyes desperate.

'Don't say it, kitten.'

'Say what?' she asked shakily, stunned by the pain and misery in his face.

'Goodbye.'

'Goodbye?' What was he talking about?

'I need you.' He lifted his hands and then let them fall back by his side as his eyes searched hers across the room. 'I need you more than I've ever needed anyone in my life. You *are* my life.' He shook his head savagely. 'I know you are the one who has been hurt, who needs someone strong to lean on, to protect you, but dammit, I'm falling apart inside. I eat you, think you, breathe you, sleep you. You feature in every little thing I do, every thought I think. I can't go on like this——' He stopped abruptly. 'Hell, Kit, I didn't mean to say——' He stopped again.

He needed *her*? Not Gerard, she thought as her stunned eyes searched his face. But it was true. As she held the beautiful gold-brown gaze she saw he was hurting too, that a pain as deep as any she had felt had marked his face. How could she not have understood? she asked herself brokenly as tears began to run in rivulets down her face. How could she have kept them apart for a minute? He needed her, wanted her, *her*. When he looked at her he didn't see someone unworthy, unlovable. He didn't see her as she saw herself, as she had been taught to see herself all through her childhood. *He loved her.* 'You need me?' Her lips formed the words but they were a light breath on the air. 'You really need me?' she asked more strongly, as a joy more piercing than any pain melted the fear and hurt.

'So much.' He was watching her, his eyes searching her face, unsure of her reaction. 'But I can wait, I can be patient——'

'I can't.' And still he hesitated, unable to believe what she was telling him.

'I want you as my wife, kitten,' he said slowly. 'I want you to join yourself with me. I want you to trust me, to understand that I'm there for you no matter what, but I know it will be hard for you. I can wait for physical love, if that's what you want, however long——'

'How long does a special licence take?' she asked softly as the tears still continued to fall.

'A special licence?' And then, at last, he was at her side gathering her into his arms and smothering her face with kisses as he groaned her name against her lips.

'I love you, I love you,' she said over and over again so that he would know, *really* know.

'And I love you.' He raised his head briefly to look down into her red, sticky, tear-streaked face. 'I always will.'

'I know,' she said quietly, lifting her hand to his hard tanned cheek, and it came to her in a blinding flash of relief that she *did* know. Finally. She would never doubt the depth of his understanding, his compassion, again. As Emma had said, they didn't come gift-wrapped like him too often and she wanted this gift, oh, she did.

'Why the Mona Lisa smile?' he asked softly as he looked down at her, a wealth of love in his eyes, and as she told him he gave a grin that was pure wickedness. 'I like your Emma,' he said with satisfied male arrogance. 'It's only her encouragement that gave me the hope to think I still had any chance at all.'

'You've been talking to Emma?' she asked in surprise.

'Of course.' He hugged her close to him, taking her mouth in a long hard passionate kiss that made her toes curl, before burying his face in the soft silky skin of her neck with a smothered groan. 'I could eat you alive,' he muttered gruffly. 'I don't know if this cosy Christmas is going to be such a good thing after all. I might be a gibbering idiot at the end of it. Restraint might be good for my soul but there are certain other parts of my anatomy that aren't controlled so easily.' He kissed her again, his hands warm and dangerously sensual as they moved beneath the silk of her pyjamas to the swell of her breasts. She shuddered at his touch and he stopped instantly, looking down at her as he drew away.

'It's all right, I know all this is new to you, don't be frightened.'

'I'm not *frightened*,' she said softly, feeling bereft as the warmth of his body left hers and more than a little put out.

'You aren't?' he asked delightedly, enchanted by her candour.

She shook her head slowly, her eyes slumberous. 'I think it's time I unwrapped that package,' she said softly. 'I've waited too long for this particular gift as it is.' And all he could do was agree.

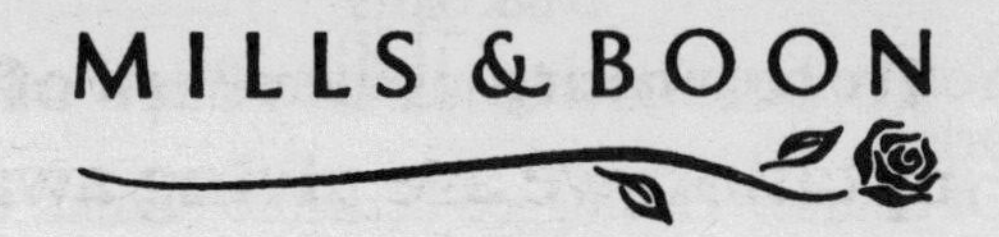

Next Month's Romances

Each month you can choose from a wide variety of romance with Mills & Boon. Below are the new titles to look out for next month.

THE HEAT OF PASSION	Lynne Graham
SWEET SINNER	Diana Hamilton
UNWANTED WEDDING	Penny Jordan
THE BRIDE IN BLUE	Miranda Lee
FAITH, HOPE AND MARRIAGE	Emma Goldrick
PS I LOVE YOU	Valerie Parv
PARTNER FOR LOVE	Jessica Hart
VOYAGE TO ENCHANTMENT	Rosemary Hammond
HOLLOW VOWS	Alexandra Scott
DISHONOURABLE SEDUCTION	Angela Wells
TEMPTATION ON TRIAL	Jenny Cartwright
TO TAME A TEMPEST	Sue Peters
POTENT AS POISON	Sharon Kendrick
SHORES OF LOVE	Alex Ryder
DANGEROUS ATTRACTION	Melinda Cross
PASSIONATE RETRIBUTION	Kim Lawrence

Available from WH Smith, John Menzies, Volume One, Forbuoys, Martins, Woolworths, Tesco, Asda, Safeway and other paperback stockists.

To celebrate 10 years of Temptation we are giving away a host of tempting prizes...

10 prizes of FREE Temptation Books for a whole year

— plus —

10 runner up prizes of Thorntons delicious Temptations Chocolates

Enter our Temptation Wordsearch Quiz Today and Win!

10th

All you have to do is complete the wordsearch puzzle below and send it to us by 31 May 1995.

The first 10 correct entries drawn from the bag will each win 12 month's free supply of exciting Temptation books (4 books every month with a total annual value of around £100).

The second 10 correct entries drawn will each win a 200g box of Thorntons Temptations chocolates.

I	F	G	N	I	T	I	C	X	E
A	O	X	O	C	A	I	N	S	S
N	O	I	T	A	T	P	M	E	T
N	B	V	E	N	R	Y	N	X	E
I	R	O	A	M	A	S	N	Y	R
V	C	M	T	I	U	N	N	F	U
E	O	H	U	O	T	M	V	E	T
R	N	X	U	R	E	Y	S	I	N
S	L	S	M	A	N	F	L	Y	E
A	T	O	N	U	T	R	X	L	V
R	U	O	M	U	H	I	A	A	D
Y	W	D	Y	O	F	I	M	K	A

TEMPTATION
SEXY
FUN
EXCITING
TENTH

ROMANTIC
SENSUOUS
ADVENTURE
HUMOUR
ANNIVERSARY

PLEASE TURN OVER FOR ENTRY DETAILS

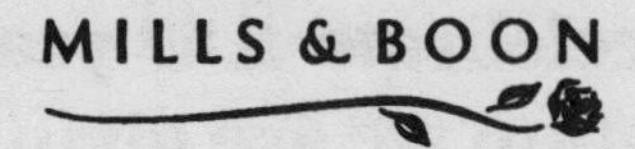

HOW TO ENTER

10¢

All the words listed overleaf below the wordsearch puzzle, are hidden in the grid. You can find them by reading the letters forward, backwards, up and down, or diagonally. When you find a word, circle it or put a line through it.

Don't forget to fill in your name and address in the space below then put this page in an envelope and post it today (you don't need a stamp). Closing date 31st May 1995.

Temptation Wordsearch,
FREEPOST,
P.O. Box 344,
Croydon,
Surrey
CR9 9EL

COMP395

Are you a Reader Service Subscriber? Yes ☐ No ☐

Ms/Mrs/Miss/Mr ______________________

Address ______________________

____

______________________ Postcode ______________________

One application per household. You may be mailed with other offers from other reputable companies as a result of this application.
Please tick box if you would prefer not to share in these opportunities. ☐

mps MAILING PREFERENCE SERVICE

DMA